The Bodyguard's Fake Bride

Books by Elle E. Kay

Faith Writes Publishing

ENDLESS MOUNTAIN SERIES:
Shadowing Stella
Implicating Claudia
Chasing Sofie

THE LAWKEEPER SERIES:
Lawfully Held
A K-9 LAWKEEPER ROMANCE
Lawfully Defended
A S.W.A.T. LAWKEEPER ROMANCE
Lawfully Guarded
A BILLIONAIRE BODYGUARD LAWKEEPER ROMANCE

Lawfully Taken
A BOUNTY HUNTER LAWKEEPER ROMANCE
Lawfully Given
A CHRISTMAS LAWKEEPER ROMANCE
Lawfully Promised
A TEXAS RANGER LAWKEEPER ROMANCE
Lawfully Vindicated
A US MARSHAL LAWKEEPER ROMANCE

THE BLUSHING BRIDES SERIES:
The Billionaire's Reluctant Bride
The Bodyguard's Fake Bride

STANDALONE NOVELLAS:
Holly's Noel
Painting the Sunset Sky (coming soon)

The Bodyguard's Fake Bride

Elle E. Kay

FAITH WRITES PUBLISHING
Benton, Pennsylvania

FAITH WRITES PUBLISHING
266 Saint Gabriels Rd
Benton, PA 17814

ISBN: 978-1-950240-15-9

This book is dedicated to my great-grandparents, John and Margaret Ewing, who instilled in our family a love for our Scottish heritage.

Chapter 1

Amy stabbed her pinkie on a thorn tossing the bouquet of black roses in the trash. Leaning back in her leather desk chair, she sucked on her injured finger.

Taking a deep breath, she bent forward and pressed the button to listen to her voice mail. The familiar voice left a hollow feeling in the pit of her stomach. She pressed the number three on her phone to delete the message and move on to the next one.

Zach. He needed to meet with Seamus McPherson. The feeling in her stomach turned to flutters. Seamus had returned to Southern California. Zach rarely made last-minute schedule changes, so whatever he wanted to see her former bodyguard about, it must be important. Opening her boss' calendar, she entered the appointment he'd requested and buzzed their shared assistant, Marjorie.

"Zach had a sudden schedule change; can you reschedule his appointments for the rest of the day?"

"Sure thing." Marjorie's deep smoker's voice crackled over the intercom.

Amy hadn't seen or heard from Seamus since he'd returned to Virginia nine months earlier.

She couldn't fathom what this meeting could be about. Unless— No. She dismissed the idea before it could take root. Seamus wouldn't consider taking the opening as their new head of security. His job with Garrison Securities was glamorous and exciting. He had no reason to leave their employ. Besides, Zach wouldn't poach employees from his good friend, Grayson.

Her cell buzzed, and she clicked the green button to answer Zach's call. "What's up, boss?"

"Did you get my message to cancel my lunch appointment and pencil in McPherson?"

"What do you think?"

"Good." He chuckled. "I'll need you at that meeting, Ames. Can you get us a table at Spago?"

"You're kidding, right?"

"I know you can do it. You're a miracle worker."

"I'll give it a shot. Do you have a second choice if I can't make it happen?"

"You always get me my first choice."

She tapped her fingernails on her desk. "Zach, seriously. Give me a second choice."

"You pick. Addison's pinching me, I have to go."

Amy smiled as she pictured Zach's wife hassling him to hang up the phone. He was a workaholic, but Addy did her best to keep him focused on what mattered most. "I'll see you in a couple of hours."

Getting Zach a table at Spago would be easy compared to sitting at the same table as Seamus.

Hopefully, she could avoid making a fool of herself. Again. His coppery hair, olive-green eyes, brawny physique, and Scottish brogue turned her insides to mush, but he had more than good looks going for him. She'd fallen for him during their long talks when she'd gotten to see beneath his tough facade to the man underneath. She'd had a ridiculous crush on him, but he'd left. He hadn't made her any promises, but she'd mistakenly believed their feelings were mutual and that they'd grown close over the weeks they spent together. Then one night he'd kissed her. She'd thought it was the start of a romance, but it was the last time she'd seen him.

Four hours later, Amy settled in beside Zach across from Seamus in the limousine. She tried not to meet Seamus' eyes, for she knew the second she did, she'd melt and be useless to her boss for the remainder of the meeting.

If Seamus took a job with Fractal, she'd have to work closely with him every day, and she couldn't even be in the same vicinity as him without flushing, so having him at work would be a monumental challenge. Zach had to know that. He wouldn't consider a move like that before asking her.

Zach's hand closed over her arm, and she turned to face him. "Where'd you go?" he asked.

She pulled her arm away and shook her head. "Sorry, I was lost in thought."

"I was telling Seamus how you managed to get us a table at Spago despite the short notice."

"It helps that you're a frequent diner there. Your

name recognition doesn't hurt either, but I don't think that type of thing would impress Seamus. He seems more like a hamburger joint kind of guy."

Seamus grinned. "Aye. Right ye are." His low bass voice rumbled through her. She glanced his way through lowered lashes. Oh, to have a man like him take an interest in her. It would be best if she could forget him. He obviously had no interest in her. If he'd been attracted to her, he would've stuck around when she'd practically gift-wrapped her heart and handed it to him. No. She needed to put away any fantasies she harbored and focus on getting through this lunch meeting.

Seamus stared at the bonnie lass seated across from him. He'd only accepted this job interview so he could see her again. Nothing had changed. She didnae share his dreams, so he shouldn't be entertaining thoughts of spending time wi' her. Despite that, he'd returned to California, and it wisnae because he had a burning desire to work for Fractal Enterprises.

He shouldn't stare, but he coudnae help himself. He noticed the curve of her lips as she laughed and admonished himself for studying her so closely. His hands itched to reach out to her. When he saw Zach place his hand on her, he had an ungentlemanly urge to batter him.

The driver parked the limo and came around to open the doors. Seamus waited for Amy to get out and joined her on the sidewalk. His hand moved automatically to the small of her back to guide her inside. Leaning down, he whispered into her ear. "How about joining me for a burger tonight?"

When she turned to face him, he saw that her smile reached her eyes. "I'd like that."

He leaned closer to her. "Seven o'clock?"

"Perfect."

A slow smile formed. All he had to do was get through this meeting, and he could spend the evening alone wi' Amy.

Amy picked at her endive salad while listening to Zach grill Seamus about his work experience, his willingness to travel, and his personal habits. To call it a thorough interview would be an understatement. There were a few times when she felt she should walk away and give them some privacy to talk 'guy stuff,' but Zachary counted on her to be by his side for all important meetings and interviews. He didn't trust himself to remember key details and knew that she always had his back. She wondered how he could be so oblivious to her feelings for Seamus. She should've asked him to bring Marjorie to this meeting instead of her. Yet, if she hadn't come along, she wouldn't have gotten the invitation to dinner. A smile touched the corners of her lips, and she snuck a glance at Seamus.

"If you were hired, how soon could you start?"

Zach scooped up his last scallop and shoved it in his mouth before pushing his plate away.

Seamus choked on his water. After a minute he regained his composure. "I'm not certain I'd take the job, Mr. Williams. Tis a possibility but not a forgone conclusion."

"Please call me Zach. Would you seriously consider turning down a job with Fractal Enterprises?"

"Aye. I micht."

"I'd make it worth it for you."

"How do ye propose to do that?"

"Money."

"I earn enough wi' Garrison Securities, and money wouldn't convince me to leave."

His hands formed a steeple and he pressed his lips together in a tight line. "I'm surprised you agreed to the interview if you weren't interested in more money."

"I had other business 'ere, and Grayson asked me to come."

"Gray knew you were coming here to interview for this position?"

Amy's hand flew to her throat and her eyes widened.

"Aye. Of course."

"I wasn't aware."

"I would nae have spoken wi' the headhunter if it had nae been for Gray's pressure."

"Why would Gray be willing to give you up?"

"Apparently, he considers ye a good friend and yer safety matters to him."

Zach's face turned red. "Hmm."

"Feeling guilty for interviewing me wi'oot talking to him first?"

"Yes."

Amy's eyebrows shot up, and she frowned. She'd never have believed that Zach would interview his friend's employee without talking to him first had he not admitted as much.

"Don't let it bother ye. Call him. He'll tell ye there isnae anything to feel guilty about." Seamus chuckled. "My being 'ere is mostly Gray's idea. He knows I've been itching to come back this way, so when the job came up, he thought I micht be the best fit from his security staff."

"What business did you have in So-Cal?"

He glanced over at her. "Personal business."

She felt her face growing warm at the implication of his words. He couldn't have meant to glance in her direction. It must've been a coincidence. Why couldn't she force herself to accept that Seamus didn't feel the same way about her as she felt about him?

"Fair enough. I won't pry," Zach said.

Seamus pushed away what remained of his meal and sat back in his chair scrutinizing Zach.

Amy rose to her feet. "If you gentlemen will excuse me, I'll be back in a minute."

His eyes followed her shapely figure as she headed away from the table.

"I'm glad we have a minute to talk alone." Zach's voice cut through his thoughts.

"Why is that?"

"Amy is the main reason I'm hoping you'll take the job."

"Zach, dinnae play matchmaker."

"I'm not. I recognize that she's got a thing for you, but that isn't what this is about."

"Then what is it about?" He narrowed his eyes.

"You know how much Amy means to Addison and I?"

"Aye."

"Well, she's been getting strange phone calls and creepy gifts."

"And?"

"I'm convinced she has a stalker."

"Has she seen anyone following her? Identified someone?"

"No. She doesn't have any idea who the gifts or phone calls are from. She's brushing them off like they're nothing, and maybe they are harmless, but I don't want to take that chance. Amy's like family to me."

"I'm aware."

"Will you consider taking the job?'

"Guarding Amy or head of security?"

"I'm hoping you'll do both."

"How would that work?"

"If you two got married or pretended to be married, you could spend most of your time together at her place, and you'd already be in the same building every day for work, so it wouldn't be so hard to guard her while taking care of your other responsibilities. She goes to most of my meetings and on all business travel with me, so you can easily keep an eye on both of us at the same time, and of course, the rest of the security staff would be at your disposal, and you could hire any additional staff you think we need."

"Ye want me to fake a marriage wi' a woman ye admit has a thing for me?"

"It's obvious you aren't immune to her either."

"All the more reason to keep my distance."

"Please. I'd consider it a personal favor."

"Coudnae ye have asked Grayson to do this for ye?"

"His wife wouldn't have agreed to let him play the part of another woman's husband."

"Right ye are."

Amy returned from the restroom and took her seat. "Did I miss something?"

He chuckled inwardly, if she only knew how much she'd missed.

Zach's eyes drifted to Amy before focusing on Seamus. "The job is yours if you want it."

"I assume ye want the conditions we discussed to be part of the offer?"

"Yes."

"I'll accept, but only if ye'll meet a condition I

have."

"What's that?"

"I have a family reunion in two weeks. Tis a week-long affair in Scotland. I need to be present for it."

"That's your condition?"

"Aye. I'd like ye to give Amy that week off so she kin attend wi' me."

Amy stood so quickly she knocked over her chair. "I'm not going anywhere with you." She stormed toward the door but slowed her steps so she could hear what Seamus said to Zach.

"It seems I put my foot in my mouth. Will ye excuse us for a minute while I smooth this over wi' her?"

She pushed through the front doors and walked over to the limo. It wouldn't do for Seamus to know she'd been eavesdropping. It was bad enough she'd made a fool of herself in the trendy restaurant, she didn't need him to know she cared what he had to say. As things stood, they'd probably never let her make reservations at Spago again. Hopefully, Zach would forgive her imprudent outburst.

"Hey." Seamus smiled down at her when he joined her.

She glared at him. "What were you thinking in there? I agreed to burgers not to join you for a week in Scotland."

"Are we on for tonight? I kin explain then."

"I should say no."

"Ye should but won't. Ye want to know more." He reached for her hand but changed his mind halfway and dropped his own hand down to his side. "I know I'm out-of-line, but 'twas not what ye were thinking. I didn't know if I'd get another opportunity to negotiate for ye to get the time off. I've seen how hard Zach works ye, so I knew if I took the job wi'oot prearranging the trip, ye micht nae be able to get away."

"Why would you want me to go with you to Scotland?" She crossed her arms over her chest.

"I'm hoping ye'll let me explain the details over dinner. Please."

"I have a feeling I'm going to regret this, but pick me up at seven." She slid into the limo and leaned back out the door. "You'd better have a full explanation tonight."

Seamus went back into the restaurant, she assumed to straighten things out with Zach. Several minutes passed before the two men joined her in the limousine.

Zach's gaze met hers. "I've a feeling that stunt will cost me if I want to keep from being blacklisted."

"Sorry, boss."

"Don't be." He lifted her chin. "Are you okay?"

"I'm fine."

"Do you want me to punch Seamus?"

"Don't get all big brother on me." She grinned. "Besides, he'd best you in a fight." She met the gaze of the man in question. "Don't smirk. It isn't becoming."

Seamus laughed. "In case ye were wondering, yer boss agreed to give ye the time off so ye kin accompany me to Scotland."

A knot formed in her stomach. How could she respond to that? What on earth did he have in mind that he wanted to drag her across the pond?

"What I said was that you could get the time off if you wanted it, and you could go with him if you so desired. I would not be so presumptuous as to assume you would choose to go anywhere with this barbarian." Zach grinned at Seamus then leaned down and whispered in her ear. "Do you mind that I hired him? I don't think we could find a better candidate for the job."

She shook her head. How much of an impact Zach's hiring decision would have on her life remained to be seen.

"You're the best, Ames."

She looked at him through narrowed eyes. "Don't you forget it.

Chapter 2

Amy fussed with her makeup and hair, but ultimately decided to leave her hair down. There was no need to get gussied up for a casual date. She slid on a pair of jeans and a soft cotton t-shirt.

Instead of enjoying the anticipation of her date with Seamus, she stressed over his odd suggestion at lunch. Why had he asked for her to get time off to go with him to Scotland? The idea was absurd. What if he wanted her to go as an assistant? She hadn't thought of that. Her face warmed. He said it wasn't what she was thinking. It may have been innocent, and she'd made a fool of herself for no reason. Their date may not even be a real date.

She plopped down on her sofa and put her feet up on the coffee table crossing her legs at the ankles but hopped up again and straightened the throw pillows. The doorbell rang. She filled her lungs and slowly released her breath as she answered the door. Seamus' massive presence filled her foyer. His subtle spicy scent tickled her nose.

"Hey," She said.

"Hey, yersel'. Ye look bonnie tonight." He made eye contact as a slow smile formed.

Her stomach did a flip. "Let me grab my purse."

She grabbed her handbag from the counter but hurried off to her laptop when she heard it ding with a new email. It took several minutes to take care of Zach's request. Once she finished, she stepped back into the foyer and found Seamus standing by her front door shifting his weight from one foot to the other. "Sorry. I should've invited you in."

"'Tis braw."

She had no idea what he'd said, but assumed he was letting her off the hook. He stepped out her front door, and she followed.

"I'll take ye somewhere nicer than out for burgers."

She locked the front door. "Burgers are perfect."

Seamus took her hand in his and laced their fingers together. Her heartbeat sped up, and she struggled to breathe normally. He opened the passenger door of his Mustang, and she slid inside. He climbed in on the driver's side, and the air felt charged between them.

Amy focused on making conversation. "Do you think you'll take the job with Fractal?"

"I'd be a fool not to."

"Why?"

"Zach claimed that taking the job would put me in close proximity wi' ye on a daily basis."

"It will."

"I'd like that."

"What sparked your sudden interest? You had no interest in me when you were here before, so why the change of heart."

"Is that what ye think? That I didnae have an interest in ye?"

"I didn't exactly hide my attraction to you." She looked down at her hands and then back up at him. "I thought we'd formed a friendship, and believed it might lead to more, but after we kissed, and I never heard from you again, it became rather clear that you weren't interested. So, what am I supposed to think now that you're back?"

"I noticed ye." His knuckles tightened on the steering wheel. "I tried not to, but I coudnae get ye out of my head, so I returned."

"You came back for the job interview."

He pulled the car into the lot of a fifties-themed burger joint. "I came for the interview, aye." He got out of the car and walked around to get her door, but she'd already opened it and stepped out. He stood in front of the open door effectively pinning her up against the car. "I was only interested in the job because I knew 'twas a chance to be close to ye."

"And what happens if you take the job, we go out a few times, and you lose interest?"

"That won't happen." A muscle jumped in his jaw.

"You left before. When you get bored with me, are you going to leave Fractal, or will I be forced to continue working with you?"

He backed away from the car door, waited for her to step away from it, then closed it and hit the lock button. "I'm sorry I left."

"Don't be. You didn't owe me anything then, and

you don't owe me anything now." She flipped her hair over her right shoulder. "I'm simply trying to understand what's going on here."

They walked into the restaurant and took a booth in the back corner. She slid in across from him. A waitress came to the table with menus and took their drink orders. He ordered them each a milkshake.

"How did you know to get me a butterscotch milkshake?"

"I may not have let on, but I paid attention to every detail when I was assigned to guard ye."

"I'm not sure how I'm supposed to feel about that."

"I hope ye'll understand that I cared. Even if I didnae let on. So, about Scotland…"

"I'm curious, how did you end up with an Irish name if you're Scottish?"

"I'm Scottish and Irish. My mother is Scottish. My father is Irish."

"How shocking."

"Twas. Irish Catholic. Scottish Presbyterian. Completely scandalous."

She laughed, but when her eyes met his, she saw a sadness that wasn't there before. "Wait. You're serious?"

"Twas a muckle deal at the time. And when they raised us children away from both churches it caused their families to disown them for a time. Thankfully, they've since smoothed things over and all is calm. For the most part anyway."

The waitress set their milkshakes down and took

their orders.

Amy took a sip. "Are you serious? Their families disowned them?"

"Aye, sometimes religious folk are more concerned wi' traditions than they are wi' God. To them, my parents raising us away from their churches was a betrayal, but all this is in the past. Yer asking questions about my heritage to avoid discussing coming wi' me to Scotland."

"Fine. Let's discuss it." She furrowed her brow. "As much as I want an explanation for why you asked Zach to give me time off for a trip to Scotland, I don't know if I'm prepared to hear the reason."

"I hoped ye micht consider coming along as my bride."

She choked on her milkshake. "We're not married."

He pulled out a ring box. "We kin fix that."

She opened her mouth to speak but closed it again to keep herself from saying something she might regret.

He got down on one knee and opened the ring box. "Amy Anderson, will ye be my pretend wife?"

The diamond solitaire sparkled up at her. She loved the simplicity of it. "You bought a ring to propose a fake marriage?"

"Aye, I bought a ring." He grimaced. "Please say aye, so I kin get up off the floor."

"I'm not agreeing to fake marry you after one date. Get up already." She frowned. "I'm going to need you to elucidate this weirdness, too."

He set the ring box between them and sat back down in his seat.

"All this is to deceive who exactly?"

"Promise not to get angry?"

"No. Absolutely not." She glared at him and placed both hands flat on the table. "That is a promise I'm not about to make."

"Zach wants us to fake a marriage, so I kin better protect ye from yer stalker."

"I should've known Zachary was behind this." She sighed. "I honestly believed this was a date. That you liked me."

"It was. It is." Seamus raked a hand through his hair. "I do."

"How can you claim that when you just told me it was all Zach's idea?"

"The fake marriage thing is his idea. The date was my own."

"How did you find out about the job with Fractal?"

"A headhunter."

"That Zach sent to you."

"Aye. I imagine so."

"It all comes back to him."

"I'm 'ere and I want to do this. I want a second chance to get to know ye better and being yer fake husband will make it easier."

"Whatever. I'll do it. I guess."

"Ye will?"

"Only because once Zach gets something in his head, he doesn't let it go, so it'll be simpler for me to accept it than to fight it. Besides, I want the time off, and I've always wanted to see Scotland."

"I could kiss ye right now."

"Don't you dare."

"How are we going to fool yer stalker into thinking we're married if ye wilnae let me kiss ye?"

"I don't think the guy is a danger. This whole plan is ridiculous."

"Even so, we should make it seem real."

"I guess we'll have to make-believe that one of us isn't fond of public displays of affection."

"Fine." He grinned. "That'll have to be ye." He reached over and caressed her ring finger before sliding the diamond ring into place. "Are ye certain ye dinnae want to seal our agreement wi' a kiss?"

She leaned back in her seat and picked up her milkshake. "You should count your blessings that I haven't tossed this milkshake in your lap."

Amy sat propped up in bed reading her Bible. She rummaged through her nightstand and found a bottle of Tums. She shouldn't have agreed to Zach's crazy fake marriage scheme. They shouldn't deceive others even for a good cause. She drew her knees up to her chest. It would be best to tell Seamus she changed her mind and refuse to go along with the plan, but she wanted to spend time with him. They had less than two weeks until the trip to Scotland, but it was possible that they'd get her admirer to back off beforehand. Then there would be no need for her to tag along with Seamus on his family reunion. It would be a disappointment since she was looking forward to the trip.

She wanted a real relationship with him. He couldn't have meant what he'd said about returning to California for her. No. She refused to fall for his stupid line about returning for her no matter how much she wanted it to be true.

She hoped he wouldn't be too disappointed when he discovered they wouldn't be sharing a bed. She'd learned to have more respect for herself than to crawl into bed with any man who showed an interest. She would wait until she had a real ring on her finger. As the temple of the Holy Ghost, she wouldn't defile herself by sleeping with Seamus or any other man.

The guilt clawed up her spine and refused to let go. Lying was as much a sin as fornication, and she planned to spend the next several weeks or possibly even months perpetrating a fraud. She closed her Bible and put aside the thought. Her intentions were good, and she'd already agreed to the plan. It would be impossible to back out gracefully now. Her fake wedding was happening in two days' time.

Seamus paced as he waited for Amy to come out of her office. He coudnae believe they were going through wi' this ridiculous fake wedding scheme. He shouldn't go through wi' it, but he wanted to keep her safe, and Zach was correct. Living together as a married couple would be the easiest way for him to guard her. If her stalker got caught quickly, it could ruin his plans for getting to know her better, but it would be good to get her out of harm's way. Then he could focus on courting her instead of protecting her.

Amy emerged from her office looking polished and professional in a black pencil skirt and red blouse. Her hair was up in a bun of sorts wi' a chopstick sticking into it. He itched to reach up and take down her hair, so it could fall down her back, but he stuffed his hands in his pockets instead.

They'd had an early morning meeting wi' the boss who wanted to ensure things ran smoothly the two days Amy would be out of the office. It hadn't taken long for Seamus to discover that Zach was an exacting boss. He demanded every moment of Amy's time, and he wisnae much easier on his other employees. He'd had barely an instant to chat wi' his bride-to-be as she showed him around the office earlier that week. The rest of their communication had been done by email or in brief snippets before and after business meetings.

Zach insisted on helping him plan an elaborate ruse of a fake wedding despite Seamus' suggestion that they simply tell people they'd gotten married at one of those Vegas wedding chapels.

Amy cocked her head to the side, and he realized he'd been lost in thought while she stood there waiting for him.

"Where are yer bags, lass?"

"In my office."

"I'll grab them."

"Thanks." She bit her lip and smoothed down the front of her skirt.

"My vehicle is waiting near the elevator in the garage."

"I hope you don't expect my bags to fit in your Mustang."

"Naw. I brought the   Lincoln Navigator."

"I didn't know you had one." She tilted her head to the side.

He got her bags and walked behind her to the elevator that led to the garage. Once inside the elevator, he briefly made eye contact wi' her before looking away. "We're doing this."

"It seems that way." She tapped her index finger against her bottom lip.

"Are ye nervous?" He cleared his throat and stared at the closed elevator doors.

"Nothing to be nervous about," she said, but her voice came out in a higher pitch than usual.

The elevator doors opened, he waited for her to step off, and then followed. He set the bags down near the back of the SUV and opened the passenger door for her before loading the bags. He slid behind the wheel and drove them to the airport where Garrison Securities kept their private jet. When they drove up, Amy lifted an eyebrow? "This isn't our plane."

"Tis Grayson's."

"You quit and he lends you his private jet?"

"Aye." He opened his door and headed around the

car to get her door. "Gray and Jenna are going to fly to Maui wi' Zach and Addison, so he's letting us use it."

"He sounds like a great boss." She ascended the stairs to the plane, and he followed.

"He is."

"Why would you leave his employ?"

"I told ye why."

"I'm smart enough not to have believed that line of malarkey." She lifted her chin.

He placed his hand on the small of her back and guided her to a comfortable seating area. Once she sat, he took the seat beside her. "Ye'll come to learn my words were honest."

She stared into his eyes as if searching for the truth in their depths.

He glanced away. "I'm feeling guilty about lying to everyone."

"Then why are we doing this?"

"Because I dinnae think I kin get ye to agree to marry me for real in the next few hours."

"You've got that right."

"Then deception is the best way to get yer stalker to back off or to make a bold move, so we kin catch him."

"He's harmless."

"We won't be taking that chance."

She glanced out the plane's window.

He took her hand in his and turned it over in his lap, tracing the lines in her palm. "Are ye looking forward to our wedding?"

"It isn't exactly what I had in mind for my first trip down the aisle." She looked down at their hands, and his fingers stilled.

"I'm sorry."

"Don't be. You're just doing your job."

She was so much more than an assignment to him, but he knew he shouldn't be pursuing a relationship wi' her. Dating someone more devoted to their job than anything else would bring nothing but problems. He'd prayed night after night for his feelings for her to go away, but they remained as strong as ever. What more could he do? When the headhunter sought him out to interview for the job with Fractal and Gray encouraged him to go, he came back to see if he and Amy could make a relationship work. He'd spent nine months trying to forget her, but she'd haunted his dreams. There was no other woman for him, so he'd finally made his move. Now, if she rejected him, he'd have to accept her decision. Taking a chance on her was worth the risk. He prayed his heart would recover if she chose her work with Zach over him. He needed time to convince her, and although his uncle wisnae well, he was still alive. He didnae need to return to Scotland quite yet.

"Do you want to talk about whatever is bothering you?" Amy's eyes searched his face.

He refused to meet her gaze. "Nae."

"What would you like to talk about?"

"We could get to know each other better."

"We know each other plenty well."

"Naw. We only know what we let each other see.

Nobody will believe we're married if we cannae answer simple questions about each other wi' some depth."

"What do you want to know?"

"I know yer from Iowa. What was life like for an Iowa farm girl?"

"Much the same as it is for most farm girls, I imagine. There was always work to be done. We went to church twice on Sundays, and we worked hard all week long. When I was old enough to rebel, I did. I moved to California with dreams of becoming an actress. It didn't take long for me to discover the futility of my ambitions. Thankfully, Zachary offered me a job, and the rest is history."

"Ye had a crush on him, didnae ye?"

"For the first few years we worked together, yes, I did."

"What changed?"

"He never noticed me. Eventually, I gave up." She gave him a sideways glance. "When he got married, I moved on."

"I'm certain he noticed ye."

"He did not."

"Ye thought I didnae notice ye, and ye coudnae have been more wrong."

"You sent mixed signals. One minute you looked at me with interest, and the next you were cold and distant."

"I was a fool. I'm sorry. I'm sure Zach noticed ye, too. Perhaps he was afraid to get involved wi' his assistant and ruin a good working relationship."

"I suppose that's possible."

"Ye must realize how beautiful ye are?"

Her cheeks colored. "I'm not beautiful."

"Yer drop-dead gorgeous. There isnae a man alive who hasn't noticed ye."

"I recognize a canned line when I hear one."

"Someone must've hurt ye. I don't know who, but I hope to someday get the opportunity to throttle the man."

"I've been hurt by more than one man, Seamus." Her smile wavered, and she avoided eye contact. "Besides revenge won't repair the damage to my heart or make me less cynical."

He opened his mouth but closed it again wi'oot asking if he'd been one of the men who'd hurt her. He shook his head. "Ye aren't cynical."

A glint shone in her dark eyes when she raised them. "What makes you think I'm not?"

"Ye would nae have agreed to go out for burgers wi' me."

She gave him a half smile. "I'll give you that." He laced his fingers through hers, and she allowed the contact. "I wanted to trust you, so I took a chance, but it was ruined when I found out Zach was behind the whole scheme." She snatched her hand back and dug out her laptop.

He leaned forward in his seat and interrupted her before she had the chance to immerse herself in her work for the remainder of the flight. "I asked ye to dinner before Zach informed me about the stalker or his fake marriage plan. None of that came up until ye left the table."

"You made that whole plan in less than five minutes?"

"We did." He grinned. "Give me a few days to prove it to ye. I'll make up for leaving before."

"You can't make up for it, but you could stick around this time."

"I will. I promise."

Her eyes were sad when they met his. "Don't make promises you don't intend to keep."

Chapter 3

Once they disembarked in Maui, he grinned. "I'll never tire of Hawaii."

"It's paradise for sure." She glanced around. "It was nice flying all the way here without Zach."

"Don't get too excited. He and Gray will be joining us shortly wi' their wives."

"How shortly?"

"In a couple of hours. Do ye think anyone would believe ye got married wi'oot Zach present?"

"Wouldn't my parents be more important people to have present for my wedding?"

"I think tis more believable that ye would get married wi'oot them than wi'oot yer boss."

She laughed. "You may be right."

He led her to a waiting car and opened the door before climbing in beside her and directing the driver to take them to their hotel. "Zach offered up his private island for our wedding and honeymoon, but I thought a public place would be better. We kin be certain that photographs will be taken of Zachary Williams that will get our wedding to make the news."

"Zach doesn't always make the news when he attends a private affair."

"Grayson has something outlandish planned. It'll be on all the news platforms."

"Are you serious?"

"Aye."

When the car pulled up outside of the posh resort, he didnae wait for the driver to open his door, exiting the vehicle, he hurried around to Amy's side. Placing his hand on the small of her back, he guided her to the counter so they could check in. "We have a suite booked. McPherson."

The woman tapped on her keyboard and then activated two key cards and handed them to them. "Congratulations, you two. I understand your wedding is on the beach at sunset tonight."

"Aye. Thank ye."

Amy remained quiet until they were inside the elevator. "I shouldn't have let you schedule our wedding for the same day as our six-hour flight here."

"Lighten up. Tis make-believe. Ye dinnae have to be at yer best."

"You said there would be cameras."

"Ye always look lovely, would ye please calm yersel'?"

"Don't tell me to calm myself." She scowled at him.

The elevator doors opened, and they found their room. She entered the keycard into the slot and pushed open the door. "Wow. Are you sure this isn't Zach and Addison's room?"

"Tis the honeymoon suite."

"She took in the king-sized bed, the seating area, and the hot-tub tucked in the corner. Wow. It's fabulous." She grinned. "I'm taking the bed. I don't know where you're going to sleep, but it won't be with me."

"I would nae dream of trying, lass."

"I thought you said you found me attractive?"

"Verra much, but I would nae take advantage of the situation. I'm nae that kind o' guy."

"What kind of guy are you?"

"The kind who will treat ye wi' the respect ye deserve."

She looked down at the floor, and he wondered if she didnae think she deserved respect. Sharing a room wi' her this night would test his resolve, but as exhausted as they both were, they'd probably fall asleep quickly. Being in such close proximity over the coming weeks would prove far more challenging. He would need to exercise self-control around her. Who was he kidding? Self-control wisnae possible. He needed prayer. Especially now that he'd promised not to take advantage of the situation. The seductive glances she sent his way would nae make it easy.

Amy slipped into the fitted ivory satin gown. It flared out near the bottom and had tiny pearl buttons on the back. She admired herself in the full-length mirror. She'd never felt prettier than she did in that dress. What would it be like to say 'I do' to Seamus when the two of them had only had one real

31

date? Like all young girls she'd dreamed of wearing a beautiful wedding gown and marrying her handsome prince. In less than an hour she would walk down the aisle and marry Seamus McPherson. Her dream would come true, but the wedding wasn't real. It was all for her stalker who may not believe she'd gotten married anyway. Even if he did buy into the charade, they couldn't know what he would do. He could give up and go away, or he might grow bolder.

A deep groan escaped, and she pushed her feelings aside. How she felt made no difference. It no longer mattered if she was ready or not. The time had come to 'pretend' to have feelings for Seamus while stuffing her real emotions down as far as possible, so he wouldn't guess how much she wanted it all to be real. She leaned in close to the mirror and freshened her lipstick.

A knock came on the suite door, and she answered it to find Addison there. "Ready for your wedding?"

Unable to control her tears, she collapsed into a wingback chair.

"Amy? Are you all right?" Her friend handed her a tissue and knelt in front of her. "What's wrong? I thought you wanted this."

Amy swiped at her tears. "They didn't tell you?"

"Tell me what?"

"That it's all fake, Addy?"

"Zach mentioned that, but I wasn't sure I believed him knowing how you feel about Seamus."

"How am I supposed to play at being married to

him? I'll lose my mind."

"It's a perfect opportunity."

"What are you talking about?"

"If anyone can turn a fake wedding into a real marriage it's you. You've been given the gift of time with him. Now you can use it to help him fall in love with you."

"You're batty."

"If Zach and I could make it work when we married because of a childhood pact, surely you and Seamus can do the same when you're already infatuated with each other."

"He told me he took the job with Fractal to be closer to me."

"That's great!"

"I don't believe him."

"Oh."

"I'm not sure I can go through with this."

"If you don't want to go out there, I'll send everyone away, and we'll go have a quiet dinner somewhere."

"Zach, Seamus, and even Grayson Garrison went to a lot of trouble to make this wedding happen. I suppose the least I can do is show up and repeat some fake vows."

"That's the spirit, but only if you're sure?" Addy held both her hands and searched her eyes.

"I'm sure." She took in a shaky breath when the other woman released her. She stood and crossed to the bathroom for one last look in the mirror. It only took a second to fix the eyeliner she'd smudged. "Am

I presentable?"

"You look spectacular. You're going to wow Seamus."

She let out an unladylike snort. "If only."

Addy went with her out to the back of the resort where she was supposed to wait until the music started.

"I have to go sit before they start. Will you be all right?" Addison asked.

After giving her friend a weak smile and waiting for her to go sit beside her husband, she sent up a prayer for strength and prepared to walk down the aisle.

The strains of the "Wedding March" started, and she walked out onto the terrace and then down the stairs leading to the beach where their guests were assembled, and her fake husband-to-be stood next to another man in a suit. When she reached the beach, she almost fainted when her father took her arm and led her the rest of the way up the aisle between the rows of chairs assembled there. She whispered, "Daddy, I didn't know you were coming."

"Wouldn't miss my baby girl's wedding for all the world, pumpkin." He grinned.

They mustn't have told him the wedding was pretend. She searched the crowd for her mom and found her dabbing her eyes with a tissue. This wedding suddenly felt all too real. When she got a minute alone with Seamus, she'd make sure he knew how displeased she was with this turn of events.

She forced a smile as they reached the front, and

her father handed her off to Seamus. When she turned to face him, his sparkling green eyes held laughter. Fighting the urge to slap him, she focused on what the preacher said. She wondered how they'd gotten him to agree to perform a fake wedding. Stuffing down the thought, she repeated her vows.

The ceremony went by quickly as she pledged her lifelong undying love to the man standing across from her. They exchanged rings and then the preacher told Seamus that he could kiss his bride. Her groom bent to kiss her, and she gave him a look that she hoped would remind him they had a no-kissing agreement. His lips brushed lightly across hers, and even that barest touch sent tingles all the way down to her toes.

A shout came from the front row, and she turned to see Grayson punch Zach in the face. Cameras flashed all around them as he accused Zach of poaching his employee. She'd known they'd planned a spectacle but hadn't expected them to make it look so genuine. It took every ounce of self-control she could muster not to laugh at their orchestrated fight. While her groom got between the other two men and pried them apart, her mother pulled her aside. "I can't believe those men are incapable of behaving themselves at a wedding. How shameful."

"I know, Mom." She wanted to share the truth about the wedding being fake, but her mother looked so happy for her that she didn't want to ruin the moment. Her parents couldn't afford to fly to Hawaii, so she knew Zach had covered their expenses. "What did you and Daddy do about the farm?"

"Your friend, Zachary found us a reputable farm-sitter. They came all the way from Texas to take care of the critters for us."

"How thoughtful of him."

"Why didn't you inform us you were getting married?"

"It happened suddenly. A whirlwind."

"Your young man said you met when he was your bodyguard. I hadn't even known you'd needed a bodyguard."

"That was around the time Zach got married, Mom. His crazy ex-girlfriend stirred things up, but once she was arrested it blew over quickly, so there was no need to worry you about it."

"I'm glad you found such a nice boy. He seems like a gentleman." Her mother leaned in closer. "He's quite a looker, too."

Amy considered her mother's words. They were true, Seamus was a gentleman, and he was certainly good looking. Sexy even. "He's the best, Mom."

"I'm happy for you." Her mother hugged her. "You practically glow when you look at him."

She waved off the comment. "I do not."

Her mother narrowed her eyes. "You absolutely do. Make sure to save a dance for your father."

"I don't think we were planning on having dancing."

"You may want to tell that to the band that's warming up over there near the dance floor set up on the beach."

It seemed odd to be caught off-guard by so many things at her own wedding. She was always the one planning things, but Zach and Seamus had told her not to worry about a thing. "I guess we are having a reception."

"Looks that way." Her mother's forehead crinkled, and she shot a glance at the groom. "How do you not know what is happening at your own wedding?"

"I let Seamus and Zach plan everything."

Her mom took a step back and raised an eyebrow. "Seriously?"

"Since I spend my life planning things for Zach, he thought I might prefer to enjoy my wedding instead of planning it."

"That was thoughtful of him."

"Honestly, I'm beginning to regret giving up control."

"Now, that sounds more like my daughter."

Amy stood at the oceans edge, shoes in her hand letting the waves lap around her ankles.

Seamus approached her. "Be careful, ye micht get that bonnie dress wet."

"What does it matter? None of this is real."

"I'm glad yer parents made it to the ceremony."

"I'm shocked you would drag my parents into this fiasco."

"Wisnae my doing. Talk to Zach."

"You could've stopped him."

"In case ye have forgotten, my parents will be dragged into this 'fiasco' as ye called it, as well. Or did ye forget we're going to Scotland to see my family?"

"I hadn't thought about it."

"Try to remember we're doing this to protect ye, not because I'm some kind of brute who wants to take advantage of ye or upset yer parents."

"You could've told me they'd be here. I mentioned being married without them here when we arrived on the island."

"I should've said something. I'm sorry." He took one of her hands in his.

She sighed. "No. I'm the one who should apologize. I'm just overwhelmed."

"I know. Ye told me this wisnae what ye wanted for yer first trip down the aisle. I get it."

"Do you?" He couldn't possibly. He couldn't know that everything turned out exactly the way she would've wanted it. The only part of their wedding that bothered her was that it wasn't real.

"I think so." He grinned and lifted her hand, spinning her. "Would ye care to dance wi' yer groom, lass?"

"I thought you'd never ask." She smiled back at him determined to enjoy the remainder of their wedding night despite its fraudulent nature. Tonight she'd relish being Mrs. Seamus McPherson until all the guests went home and the charade was over.

Two in the morning found them sitting at a table for two. She dipped a shrimp into cocktail sauce and ate the last bite before dabbing her mouth with a napkin. Their guests had gone back to their rooms. She smiled at the beautiful man seated beside her. "Mmm. That was delicious."

"I'm glad ye enjoyed it, lassie." Seamus held his hand out to her. "Care for a walk on the beach?"

She nodded, kicked off her shoes, and placed her hand in his. Nobody remained on the beach as far as she could see. It appeared deserted. They moved closer to the ocean's edge. The lights from their hotel faded, and she enjoyed the feel of the cool sand between her toes.

She leaned sideways into him and sighed.

"Ye ken, ye dinnae have to pretend anymore. Everyone is gone."

"The wedding felt unfeigned."

"Aye. It seemed genuine.'

He stopped, released her hand, and turned her to face him. He cupped her head and ran his thumb along her jawline. Little shivers shot up her spine.

"What are you doing?"

"I'm aff to kiss ye."

"We agreed that we weren't going to do any of that."

"Are ye certain ye want to stick to that arrangement? Wi' yer permission, I would lik' to do away wi' those restrictions, Mrs. McPherson?"

Her tongue darted out and she moistened her lips. Giving her ascent would be easy. She could melt into his arms and enjoy his kisses for as long as they lasted. She wanted to be his. Body, soul, and spirit.

Then she remembered her heart and how easily he could crush it. Again. As his lips lowered to hers, she skittered away. "I can't. I'm sorry. I want to, but I can't. She ran along the beach back toward the resort.

Seamus caught up to her before she got far. "I'm sorry. I shouldn't have pressured ye. Tis just that being around ye is an unbearable temptation. I'll do better. I promise."

She nodded even as her heart reminded her, she didn't want him to keep his promise. He placed his hand on the small of her back as they approached the hotel. When they neared the back entrance, she remembered she needed to act like a newlywed and wound her arm around Seamus' waist and held onto him until they got into the elevator.

"Yer giving me mixed signals, lassie." He rubbed the stubble on his chin.

Her gaze darted around the elevator, and she took a step away from him. "I was playing it up for the staff. When we're alone, we should be more cautious."

"Yer sure that's what ye want?"

"It is." It wasn't, but she couldn't let him know she longed for his touch. It was bad enough he knew she'd spent months pining for him, he didn't need to know the depth of her feelings for him.

Seamus took a pillow from the bed and grabbed a

spare blanket from the closet. The couch in their suite wouldn't be comfortable, but he'd make do. His work as a bodyguard often meant sleeping on furniture not meant to support his 6'2" frame. He cast a furtive glance toward the bed where his bride would be sleeping. He could hear her in the bathroom changing for bed. This fake marriage thing would be the death of him. He'd understood the restrictions she'd placed on their relationship, but he'd believed she'd come around once she recognized his feelings were authentic. She hadn't. Now that they were back in their suite, reality hit hard. The bonnie lass who'd spent the night on his arm did not belong to him and likely never would.

He stretched out on the couch and pulled the blanket over him.

Five minutes later, Amy came out of the bathroom wi' her face freshly scrubbed of makeup and her silky robe tied around her waist. He fought to keep his eyes from roaming downward to admire her shapely legs.

A huge grin graced her lovely face. "You look ridiculous."

"What makes ye say that? I look the same as I did when ye left the room ten minutes ago."

"I meant the way your legs are hanging over the edge of the couch."

"There isnae much I kin do about my height."

"No. I suppose not." She moaned. "You take the bed. I'll sleep on the couch."

"I'm not letting ye sleep on the couch."

Amy rolled her eyes and stalked over to the bed. She gathered up a bunch of pillows and built a barrier down the middle of the bed. "If you stay on the window side, you can sleep in the bed."

He jumped at the chance. "Aye. Perfect."

"You can't sleep on the couch when you don't fit. How much good will you do as my bodyguard if you throw out your back."

He hoped her concern for him was more personal than she'd made it sound, but he said nothing more. Two seconds later he'd climbed under the covers and turned to face the window. "Thank ye. This is much better."

An hour passed before he heard the steady breathing that signaled she'd fallen asleep. He lifted himself up to a sitting position and watched her sleep. Devoid of make-up, wi' her hair splayed out on the pillow, she was more lovely than ever before. He forced himself to look away and lie down facing away from her. He shouldn't be obsessing over his bride. She wisnae truly his wife, and no matter how much hc longed for her, she'd made it clear she wanted him to keep his distance. He wisnae to touch her unless it was necessary to help them make their marriage look real to outsiders.

Chapter 4

Amy woke up sometime during the night and discovered she'd pushed past the pillows and moved closer to Seamus. They weren't touching, but if she hadn't woken up when she did, they would've been soon enough. She pushed down the panic rising inside her and moved back to her own side of the bed. Thankfully, they were only staying one more night, and when they returned to So-Cal he could sleep in the spare bedroom. That would keep him at a safe distance.

When she next awoke, she threw her forearm over her eyes to block the brilliant light streaming in through the windows. They mustn't have closed the curtains the night before. Feeling next to her with her other arm, she realized Seamus wasn't beside her.

She stood and stretched before wandering over to the balcony and sliding the door open. The warm breeze caught her hair as she took in the beauty of the morning. She jumped when she realized someone was standing behind her but relaxed a fraction when she recognized Seamus' scent. His strong arm encircled her waist and his left hand splayed over her middle. She leaned back into his muscular frame delighting in the intimacy of his embrace.

"Good morning, lass. I brought coffee."

"Mmmm."

She turned in his arms and lifted her face upward, but when he lowered his lips to meet hers, she pulled away. "I'm sorry. I need to brush my teeth. I'll be back." The sound of his groan reached her as she hurried into the restroom. She wanted to give in to temptation, and let herself fall for Seamus, but she couldn't. Doing so would guarantee another broken heart at the end of their arrangement. If he wouldn't think about the future, she would. Someone had to keep a level head.

Once she'd showered and brushed her teeth, she threw on a lightweight cotton sundress and rejoined Seamus on the balcony.

He sat at the table sipping his coffee. "That took a long time."

"I decided to shower while I was in there."

"You were avoiding me." He handed her a coffee. "Two creams and one sugar?"

"Perfect." She sat down and took a long sip.

"What would ye like to do today?"

"Lounge on the beach."

"We could go hiking if ye'd like."

"I don't know."

"How many times will ye get to come to Maui while yer young and healthy enough to hike to some of the world's most breathtaking waterfalls?"

"Fine. We'll hike."

"Ye may want to put on something more appropriate. Did ye bring practical shoes?"

"No. I did not."

"We'll stop and buy some."

"You really want to hike?"

"Ye'd regret it if ye didnae get to see at least one of the many natural wonders 'ere on the island."

"I'll go, but not on one of those ten-mile hikes."

"We'll take an easy trail."

She stood and faced him. "I don't believe you."

"Smart woman." He pulled her closer, and the warmth of his hand seared through the thin fabric of her dress sending a jolt of electricity through her and making her toes curl. His smile slipped, and he took a step back. "Go ahead and get ready. I'm going to accompany Zachary and Addison to the airport and make certain they get off the ground safely."

"Give me a second to change, and I'll join you." She smiled and picked up her coffee.

"I'll wait right 'ere."

Three minutes later, she returned. She'd changed into lightweight capris and a t-shirt.

"I'm glad ye decided to join me. it will save time."

"In a hurry?"

"Naw, but I do want to make the most of our remaining time on the island."

Seamus closed the room door and they both stepped onto the elevator. She twisted her ponytail and caught her bottom lip between her teeth.

Turning to face her, he asked, "Something making ye nervous, lass?"

"Not at all."

He chuckled. "Yer a terrible liar."

"Then we're going to have some trouble in the coming weeks."

"Hopefully, not everyone will see through ye as clearly as I do."

"My parents believed we were wed."

"Good enough. If ye kin fool them, ye will be able to fool most people."

"Yeah." The thought didn't please her.

Seamus draped his arm around Amy's shoulders as he watched Zach's private jet take off. The charade worked wonders. All the prominent newspapers and websites ran stories about Zach's altercation at his assistant's wedding. It would nae be long before her stalker got the news of her marriage. They'd soon learn if he would quietly go away or if he would up his game.

"Ye ready for an adventure, lass?"

She nodded and he opened the door of the rental car for her to climb in. There would be no driver for them today. He wanted her all to himself.

An hour later, they made it to the trailhead for the first waterfall on his itinerary. Noticing the broken glass in the far parking lot, he moved the car to a safer location near a shaved ice stand and paid a local boy to guard it before taking off down the trail wi' Amy reluctantly trudging along beside him.

She stooped down to tie her shoelace. "I don't know how I feel about spending our honeymoon hiking."

He grinned. "Ye'll be glad ye did."

She rolled her eyes as she stood. "How far is this waterfall?"

"Tis about a fifteen-minute hike according to the guidebook."

When they arrived at the waterfall, he climbed over some rocks to get to it and helped her to climb into the cave wi' him. They stood behind the cascade of water. "Look at that. Tis awesome, dinnae ye think so?"

"God makes some amazing things."

He stared down at her. "Aye. He does."

She turned away to face the water again. "I'm glad you convinced me to hike."

He smiled. "I would nae have let ye miss it. Wait until ye see where we're going next."

"We're going somewhere else?" She twisted the end of her ponytail around her index finger.

"Aye. That we are." He winked and started back down the path.

Amy trudged along beside Seamus as they hiked toward yet another waterfall. Her steps slowed as they tramped through the bamboo forest, and she wiped sweat from her brow. She should be on the beach sipping a virgin strawberry piña colada.

The roar of rushing water greeted her before they rounded the last corner and the mist from the falls cooled her overheated skin. The magnificent view almost made her forget how much her feet ached. She climbed up onto a rock, lay flat on her back on the warm surface, and turned her head to watch as Seamus dove into the crystal-clear water. The next thing she knew, his hand closed around her ankle. "Don't you dare!" He ignored her warning and pulled her in wi' him.

She sputtered when she reached the surface. "I'm soaking wet."

"Ye'll dry by the time we make it back to the car."

She tried to stand but couldn't reach the bottom. "How deep is this?" She looked around frantically.

His eyes searched hers. "Don't worry. I've got ye. Cannae ye swim?"

"A little."

"I'll keep ye safe, lass."

She wrapped her arms around his neck and reveled in the mixed sensations of the cool liquid and his warm body pressed against hers. Before she could get too comfortable in his arms, he lifted her up out of the water and set her back on the rock.

"You know my shoes will never dry, right?"

"Ye'll be fine. Ye have yer sandals in the car."

"Are you ready to go?" she asked.

He hauled himself up out of the water and settled in beside her on the rock. "Let's lie 'ere a moment first."

"Tomorrow we get back to the real world."

"As much as ye kin call living wi' a woman I'm pretending to be married to the real world." He chuckled.

She laid back down and turned on her side to face him. "Yeah. I guess there is that."

"Uh huh." His gaze took on an intensity as he looked into her eyes.

His wet t-shirt showed off his muscles in a way she hadn't seen before, so she forced herself to glance away, but not before he caught her looking. She saw the gleam in his eyes a moment before he took her hand in his and moved it to his chest.

She held her breath a moment, and then smiled. "You're going to get us in trouble."

"Wi' who?"

"This relationship is fake, remember?"

"Tis real to me." He spoke so quietly that his words were nearly swallowed by the roar of the rushing water.

"It's not real to me." She forced herself to remove her trembling hand from his body.

He clenched his jaw and squeezed his eyes shut.

She'd gone and done it again. Why couldn't she learn to keep her mouth shut? Maybe she should apologize. She scrubbed a hand over her face and turned to face the waterfall so she wouldn't see the hurt she knew she'd caused. As things stood, the emotional and physical distance separating them felt like a self-made prison. She had the key to release them, but she wasn't willing to do so. Things would be easier if he'd act like his old standoffish self. Then she wouldn't struggle to keep the promise she'd made to herself to protect her heart from him. It seemed that guarding her own heart meant injuring his, and she didn't want that either.

The ride back to the hotel passed in silence. Seamus held the steering wheel in a death grip. He reminded himself that he'd hurt Amy, and she needed time to learn to trust him again. He had to take things slow, or he'd scare her off for good. Winning her over would take some time. They'd had a wonderful day together, but he'd let his physical attraction get in the way, and almost lost control. He had no doubt that if he pressed her, she'd give in to his kisses, but it would be better if she came around on her own. For his plan to work, he coudnae let their physical relationship move faster than their emotional one.

She was sleeping in the passenger seat when they pulled up outside of the hotel. "Wake-up, sleepy-head."

She startled and looked up at him. "Oh. We're back. I must've fallen asleep." She waited for him to come around and open her door. He tossed the keys to the valet, and the two of them trudged into the hotel where he hit the button for the elevator.

"I must look a mess." She pulled out her scrunchie and smoothed her hair down.

"Yer lovely, as always."

"You need your eyes checked, mister."

"Mister?"

She smiled. "I like it. Makes it seem like you're older than me."

"I am."

"Are you?"

"Ten days."

"Wow. That's oddly specific."

"Dinnae ye remember? I received an in-depth briefing on ye."

"That was a long time ago."

"Not that long."

The elevator doors opened, and he took her hand as the doors closed behind him. Once they entered their room, she looked down at their joined hands, but said nothing and made no move to pull away from him.

He tucked her in to his side and kissed the top of her head. "Ye kin have first shower, lass." He watched her scurry across the room and gather up her clothes before heading into the bathroom. He went out on the balcony to wait for her to finish.

Ten minutes later, she joined him. "I'm exhausted."

"Why don't ye take a nap before dinner?"

"You wouldn't mind?"

"Why would I mind? I have to shower anyway."

When he returned from his shower, Amy slept atop the covers. An envelope lay on the floor by the door. He retrieved it and tore it open. He pulled out the note card and turned it over. The words scrawled across it said "He can't have you. You're mine." A chill ran through him and a vein pulsed in his temple. He called down to the front desk and asked if anyone had requested their room number. They couldn't answer for the previous shift but hadn't received any inquiries in the past two hours.

He decided not to mention the note to Amy until they returned to California. That way she'd be able to enjoy their last evening on the island. No sense upsetting her. Though, she hadn't seemed all that worried about her "admirer" as she called her stalker. He slid the card into his breast pocket. When she woke, he decided to visit the reception desk to ask more questions while she dressed for dinner. When he stepped into the hall, the smell of roses greeted him. There, scattered in the hallway in front of their suite, were at least two dozen black roses. He gathered the flowers up and stuffed them into a nearby trash receptacle. He would nae let the creep ruin their night. Her stalker managed to get to Hawaii much faster than they'd predicted. It should've taken him longer to see the story and get a commercial flight. Could he have an inside track on information? Was he someone that Amy, Zach, or Addison trusted? Had they invited him to their wedding? The questions swirled in his mind until he wanted to put his fist through the wall.

Never had a case felt so personal. Someone wanted to hurt the woman he cared for, and he would nae let that happen. There was no real question as to why the man had chosen black roses, but it wisnae something he was willing to dwell on.

Amy opened the door and came out looking stunning in a cocktail dress. He felt himself getting choked up but forced himself to speak. "Ye look gorgeous, lassie."

"Thanks. Is everything all right? You seem tense."

"I'm fine. I just want to get this over wi'."

Chapter 5

Seamus' words echoed in Amy's head. He wanted to get it all over with. She'd been such a fool when she'd dared to hope that he cared for her and that their sham of a marriage might mean as much to him as it did to her. They'd had a great day together, or so she'd thought, but now he wanted to get their marriage over with. She wondered if he'd gotten a phone call from a girlfriend while she showered. There could be someone waiting for him back in Virginia. He wasn't going back there now that he'd committed to taking the job at Fractal, but his girlfriend could move to California with him. He'd be staying at her place in Beverly Hills for the next week, but she didn't know where he planned to go when their marriage farce ended. She turned the options over in her mind, but all she could concentrate on was his desire to be done with her.

She got through dinner by saying as little as possible.

"Yer quiet tonight?"

"There's nothing left to say."

"What do ye mean?"

"You said everything that needed to be said earlier."

"What are ye talking about?"

She shook her head. "Don't worry about it. We'll be back in California soon, and you'll have your own space."

His brow wrinkled as he stared across at her. "When did I say I wanted my own space?"

"You didn't have to."

Standing he pushed his chair in and pulled out some bills to pay the check. He reached for her arm and drug her out of the restaurant and onto the beach. "What is yer problem tonight, Lass?"

"My problem is you."

"All of a sudden ye have a problem wi' me?" He rubbed his chin.

"Yes."

"Fine, but I have a job to do, so ye need to git over yersel' and act like a devoted bride. Kin ye do that?"

"I can act just as well as you can." She looped her arms around his neck, pulled him down to her, and kissed him with every ounce of passion she'd been holding back. Then she remembered his earlier words and backed away. "How's that for acting?"

"If that kiss was an act, lass, ye had me fooled." He cleared his throat and looked out over the ocean.

"Good. Then everyone else will believe it, too." She slid her arm around his waist and walked along the beach beside him. It was a sweet torment to be so close to him physically while building a fire-proof safe around her heart to keep him out.

Seamus balled his fists at his side. If he had a partner nearby, he'd get him to relieve him while he spent an hour or two in the hotel gym. Amy's arm hung around his waist, and she made tiny circles on his abs wi' her thumb. An hour ago, he would have believed she cared for him, but now that she'd announced her play-acting skills, he wanted to be free from her touch.

Despite his feelings, the danger she was in was genuine, and her stalker had followed her, so he couldn't abandon her now. He pulled his cell out and punched Grayson up. His former employer answered on the first ring. "Are ye still in Maui?"

"I'm here. As a matter of fact, I'm watching you now."

"Good Come meet us."

His friend walked out of the shadows and joined them on the beach. "I didnae ken ye were there. How do ye do that?"

"I'm good."

"I've never been able to get that right. People sense my presence." Seamus looked around "Where's Jenna?"

"In our room."

"Why were ye watching us?"

"A threatening call came through earlier, so I wanted to ensure your safety."

"Who took the call?"

"One of our guys we had working behind the hotel

desk."

"And?"

"A man requested your room number."

"He got it."

"What?"

"Someone slid a card under the door and left two dozen black roses in front of our room."

"I'm sorry, man. I didn't know he'd gotten into the hotel or I would've alerted you immediately."

"We're in the honeymoon suite. It micht've been a lucky guess."

"That would make sense if the hotel didn't have four honeymoon suites. None of the other honeymoon suites had issues or the hotel's head of security would've notified me."

Seamus held Amy's hand as the three of them made their way to Gray and Jenna's room. Jenna opened the door and ushered them inside. Seamus sat down on the loveseat and Amy settled in next to him.

"We should take this threat seriously." Gray sank into a chair and bent forward to get his laptop.

"What makes this one more significant than his previous gifts? He always leaves me black roses." Amy leaned into Seamus, and he pulled her closer to his side.

"The significance is that he followed you to Hawaii. It would've been difficult for him to get here that quickly unless he has access to a private plane or was already here as one of your guests. Those two scenarios make him significantly more dangerous than we initially believed him to be. You should know that the color black symbolizes death and grief and could be a threat on your life. With his gifts he's broadcasting that he'd prefer you were dead than for another man to have you," Gray said.

Seamus plucked the note card from his pocket and handed it to his friend. "That about sums up his message."

Gray scanned the card. "Let's nail this guy."

"I don't even know who this man is." Amy's hand fluttered at the base of her throat.

"Do you have any thoughts on who it may be?"

"Not a clue."

"We'll have to go over all your contacts and see if we can narrow down a list of suspects. This creep is playing for keeps and if I'm right, your life may well be in danger," Gray said.

Three hours later they'd compiled a list of every man in Amy's life. They narrowed their suspects down to five. A grocery store clerk, a barista, and three guys she'd dated. Gray ran checks on all of them.

Gray looked up from his computer. "One of your boyfriends had two priors and your coffee wizard has a prior."

"Which boyfriend?" Amy asked.

"Gary."

Seamus leaned in. "Any related crimes?"

"The boyfriend hit for domestic violence and the barista for stalking."

"Gary wasn't my boyfriend. We went on one blind

date."

Seamus nodded. "Both of those seem like promising suspects."

"Agreed. I'll find out if either one of them have been in Maui in the last twelve hours."

Gray and Jenna gathered their things, and the four of them gathered by the door.

"You'll be safer here," Gray said.

"Where will ye go?"

"We're going to book another room."

"Ye dinnae think Amy's stalker will figure all this out?"

"As long as he isn't watching us at this very moment, we should be able to pull it off. We can fly Amy home tomorrow without further incident."

"Och. We'll meet ye at yer jet first thing."

"You won't be making the drive alone. We'll have a car in front and behind."

"I'm not driving around like I'm in a presidential motorcade, Grayson. Forget it."

"Don't you want to keep your bride safe?"

Seamus crossed his arms over his chest. "Fine."

Once Gray and Jenna were gone, he turned to face Amy. "Ye should get some sleep."

"What about our stuff?"

"Gray will make certain tis packed up and wi' us on the plane tomorrow."

"What will I sleep in tonight."

He unbuttoned his dress shirt and slipped it off. "Ye kin wear this. I'll sleep in my t-shirt."

She took it from him and headed for the bathroom to change. He caught her lifting it up to her nose before she disappeared behind the door. He smiled at the gesture. She cared more than she let on. When she returned two minutes later wearing only his dress shirt, he struggled to breathe normally. The woman would look good in anything, but the intimacy of her in his shirt caused his throat to constrict and his mouth to go dry. He had to remember that she didnae want a romance wi' him. She'd made it clear that their relationship was nothing more than a performance to her. If he could keep that in mind, he micht be able to protect his heart.

The seductive smile that graced her face wisnae helping.

"Ye kin break character, lass. We're alone. Go ahead and get some sleep. We need to fly out early."

"What about you? Aren't you coming to bed?"

"I think tis best if I sleep on the couch tonight. Those pillows didnae stay put last night, and I don't trust myself to share a bed wi' ye."

"Oh. Okay."

He watched as she crawled under the covers. It would be nice to lie down beside her, but for the sake of his own sanity he needed to keep his distance.

He pulled the cushions off the couch and laid them out on the ground hoping it would be more comfortable then trying to lie on the couch. After a restless night, he rose at dawn to find Amy out on the balcony.

"What are ye daein' up?"

"I couldn't sleep." She leaned both arms on the railing and looked out over the ocean. "Why are you up?"

"Tis time to get ready to go."

"Why didn't you tell me about the flowers and card?"

"I did."

"Not until Grayson joined us." She turned to face him. "Why hadn't you already told me?"

He scrubbed his hand over his face. "I didnae want to ruin our remaining time on the island."

"Then why did you call Grayson?"

"I coudnae take yer 'acting' anymore."

"I wasn't acting." She looked down at her feet and then back up at him. "I was angry when I said that."

"If it wisnae acting, what was it? "

"My feelings for you are complicated, Seamus."

"Yer kiss meant something?"

She shook her head slowly. "I wish it didn't."

"Dinnae do that, lass."

"Do what?"

"Give me hope only to snatch it back."

"What do you mean?"

"Ye wished it didnae mean anything? Ye'd rather ye felt nothing for me?"

She shrugged.

"Are ye trying to injure me?"

She swallowed and took a step closer to him. He kissed the top of her head. "Yer everything to me, lassie. Let me keep the hope alive that my feelings will be returned."

Wrapping her slender arms around his waist, she rested her head on his chest, and he breathed in her floral scent. If he spent another full day alone wi' her, he'd lose control. It took all his self-control to take her by the arms and move her away from him. "We need to get ready to leave."

"Am I supposed to put my dress back on?"

He nodded. "Just until we get on the plane. Yer clothes will be on board, so ye kin change into something else once we get to the airport, unless ye would like me to run down to the shops and get ye something to wear?"

She shook her head. "No. I'll change on the plane."

Amy felt ridiculous leaving the hotel dressed in her cocktail dress from the night before. Anyone who saw them would think she was doing the walk of shame. They couldn't know that she'd slept separately from the gorgeous male specimen walking beside her. Most people wouldn't have blamed her if she'd have slept with him, but it went against her Christian values and though she didn't pretend to be perfect, she did her best to follow God's word.

If Seamus cared about her as much as he claimed to, then he would understand why they couldn't act on their mutual attraction. At least not without getting married for real first. She giggled at the idea.

The two of them appeared to be married to anyone else, and only a small circle of their most trusted friends knew the truth. The valet brought their car around, and Seamus held the passenger door open for her. Within seconds she noticed a car ahead of them and another behind them. "People are going to think we're important."

"Ye are important to me."

After nine months of absence from her life, Seamus had come back full force. Nothing in his demeanor seemed tentative this time. As much as she longed to trust him and let him steal her heart, she couldn't. What if he up and left again? What if she didn't measure up to his expectations for her? She couldn't take another Seamus McPherson heartbreak. She hadn't yet recovered from the first one.

She wasn't being fair to him. He hadn't given her any reason to believe that he'd wanted a romance the first time around. One dizzying kiss did not count as a promise. Their love affair had only existed in her head. Current circumstances were different. He'd made his desire to be with her abundantly clear, and she hadn't made it easy for him. She'd known her comments about acting would cause him pain, but she'd said them anyway. She'd wished immediately that she could take her words back, but like sand thrown in the wind, her words couldn't be retrieved.

They arrived at the airport and he opened her door for her. She hooked her arm through his as they walked up to Gray's jet. Gray and Jenna preceded them onto the jet.

"Your bags are on board. I had them loaded earlier. You'll find them in the bedroom." Grayson pointed to the back of the plane.

"There's a bedroom on here?"

"Didn't you show her around?" Gray lifted an eyebrow.

Seamus chuckled. "Didnae think 'twas necessary. Zach's jet must be just as luxurious."

"It is, but this one is fabulous, as well," Amy said.

Jenna stood. "Come on. I'll show you where your stuff is. I'm sure you want to get out of that dress."

"You've got that right."

Chapter 6

Seamus let Amy out of the car and placed his hand on the small of her back. He'd had two members of Fractal's security team guarding her place while they'd been in Hawaii and an advance team had checked the house earlier to make certain nothing was amiss. As they approached her front door, he reached his arm out to stop her forward progress. A package sat by the door.

Amy tilted her head to the side and touched his arm. "What is it?"

"Wait 'ere." His voice sounded cold and impersonal even to his own ears, but he coudnae help it. There was work to be done. Staying in professional mode would help him focus. He needed to forget about any romantic notions toward Amy anyway. If her intent was to get even for his leaving, he didnae need the pettiness and games. He approached the package. "Did ye order something from Dell?"

"It's a new laptop." She twisted the end of her ponytail around her finger. "In all the craziness with the wedding, I forgot I ordered it."

He inserted the key and pushed open the front door. "I find it difficult to believe Zach's perfect assistant forgot anything." He stopped in his tracks and took a step backward. "Someone is getting fired today." Amy pushed at his back trying to get into her house. He turned to face her, keeping his body between her and her house. "It would be better if ye didnae go inside."

"Why? What is it?"

She wiggled her way between him and the door frame, and her scream pierced his eardrums. He lifted her into his arms and carried her outside.

"Are ye a' richt?"

"I will be when you put me down."

Her whole body shook. He let her slide down his body until she had her feet on the ground, but he kept a firm grasp on her. "Kin I trust ye not to go inside if I release ye?"

"I need to check out the rest of the house to see if there's more damage."

"Not before I thoroughly check things out. Then we must call the police."

"The police?"

"In case ye didnae notice, there is blood all over yer living room sofa. We need to find out if tis human. The police are going to need to come out 'ere."

"Shouldn't they check it out before you go back inside."

"Aye." He gave her a half smile. "But, if I let them, they'll keep the evidence to themselves, and I won't be able to glean information from this incident."

She stared into his eyes. "You can let me go. I won't go inside until you say it's okay."

He let her go and she sat down on the front steps. He pulled out his cell and called Grayson. "We had another incident." After going over the details wi' his friend, he hung up and turned to face Amy.

Her dark eyes sparked. "He'll pay for this."

"Aye. He will."

"Why did you call Grayson? I thought you worked for Fractal now."

"Zach and I agreed to keep Garrison Securities on hand for yer protection detail."

"That's a lot of manpower to protect one woman."

"Tis no more than ye had when Zach and Addison were in danger."

"Seems like overkill."

"Not when it is a woman people care about."

"Yeah. I guess Zach does care."

How could she not realize he cared about her more than Zach did? He'd been the one to request that Garrison Securities stay on the job for additional protection but let her credit the boss. Didnae make a difference. He would catch her stalker and then go home to Scotland. He coudnae work that closely wi' her. He'd tell Zach to find someone else to be his head of security. His interest in the position had dried up along wi' Amy's affection toward him. He punched in Zach's number, and he answered on the first ring. "Do I have the power to fire people?"

After explaining the situation to Zach and spending five minutes calming the other man down, he hung up and refocused on the woman he'd sworn to protect. "How are ye holding up?"

"I'm fine."

"Do ye mind if I check things out?"

"No. Go ahead."

He did a quick walk through and didnae find anything else amiss. The furniture in the living room was dripping wi' blood, most of it splashed over the couch where she spent her evenings reading or watching television. The monster knew her routine. He'd been watching her and knew how to maximize psychological trauma.

Amy stopped pacing and faced Seamus. "If Zach offered us a wing on his estate, I don't understand why we can't stay there." She lifted her chin. Being bossed around and told what to do was getting old. She could see why Seamus didn't want them to stay at her place while it was crawling with cops, but there had to be a better option than another shared hotel room. Confined space equaled forced intimacy, and she wanted their relationship to progress naturally if it was going anywhere at all.

"We shouldn't put Zach, his wife, and all his staff at risk. it will be easier to control the situation at a hotel."

"Will we get two rooms?"

"You don't think it would be strange for newlyweds to have two separate rooms?"

"Fine, but we're stopping somewhere to pick up an air mattress. I'm not going to feel guilty for making you sleep on a tiny couch."

"I'll send someone to get one."

"Won't they be suspicious that newlyweds need them to pick up an air mattress?" She crossed her arms over her chest. "I think we should stay with Zach." She said again knowing it would annoy him.

"Are you two having an affair?" A flash of gold glinted in his green eyes.

She raised her hand to slap him, but he grabbed her wrist. "You're hurting me."

"Ye should've thought that through before ye decided to assault me."

He released her and stormed away. She followed and placed a tentative hand on his waist. "I'm sorry."

"Sure."

She rested her head against his back, and he let out a deep sigh.

"Do you think I'm the kind of woman who would fool around with a married man?"

"Nae." He turned to face her.

"Then why ask me that?"

A muscle jumped in his jaw. "Tis just that ye constantly talk about him."

"I work for him."

"Ye need more in yer life than work."

She wondered how he would respond if she told him how much she longed for him to occupy the empty space in her life. She reached up and ran her fingers through his ginger hair before turning her attention to the matching stubble on his jawline.

He growled low in his throat. "Ye better watch

yersel', lassie."

"What do you mean?"

"If ye dinnae keep yer hands to yersel', dinnae expect me to do so."

She stuffed her hands into the back pockets of her jeans. "Point made."

Seamus read through his emails while Amy showered. He called a meeting of the security staff to discuss Amy's stalker situation. They needed to figure out who was threatening her and how to stop him. He felt like a failure for allowing the man to get into the hotel and inside her home. His emotional involvement must be clouding his judgment. He cataloged the events of the past days and recognized that Amy posed too great a distraction for him. He should've refused the assignment knowing his feelings for her would prevent him from being at his sharpest.

He strolled over to the window and looked out over the city. If it wisnae for her stalker, he micht've taken her to an upscale restaurant for a nice meal. She deserved to be spoiled. Instead she'd be dining on pizza while he went to Fractal to meet wi' his security team and then accompany Zach to a meeting.

The bathroom door opened, and Amy came out wrapped in a fluffy white robe wi' a towel around her head.

"Forget yer clothes?"

"Actually, I did. Yes."

She rummaged through her suitcase collecting what she needed and shuffled back into the bathroom.

He opened an adjoining door into the next room. "Trent?"

Trent stood to his full height. "What's up?"

"I need ye to keep an eye on my wife while I meet wi' Zachary Williams."

"That's what I'm here for, boss."

"Gray is your only boss now."

"Not on this job."

"Quit it."

"I'm not complaining. He offered me your old job."

"Glad to hear how easily he replaced me." Seamus rubbed the back of his neck.

"He'd take you back anytime."

He grinned. "I'll be back late. Keep an eye on the lass."

"I'll make sure nothing happens to her while you're gone."

"Ye better."

Seamus knocked on the bathroom door and Amy opened it a crack. "I'm going out for a while. Trent is next door if ye need him."

"Where are you going?"

"I have a meeting wi' the security staff, and then I'll be attending a meeting wi' Zach so his security detail can be relieved."

"I thought Zach said to hire more people."

"I need to go through the interview process and

then do background checks on any promising candidates. We're not there yet."

"Can't Garrison Securities take care of it?"

"Tis my job, lass."

"Wait a minute, and I'll join you."

"No. Stay 'ere. Ye need to rest. Tis been a stressful day." And he didnae want to share her wi' Zach. If he brought her along, Zach would find work to keep her busy for the next four or five hours at a minimum.

"Fine. Go." She frowned. "I'll sit here and twiddle my thumbs."

Amy waited until she heard the ding of the elevator before sitting on the floor and slicing open the Dell box. She'd grabbed it as they left the house, so she could get it set up right away. A call to tech support helped her get connected to the Fractal Network.

When the door between the rooms cracked open, she startled at the handsome dark-haired man standing there.

"Sorry to bother you, ma'am. You didn't answer when I knocked."

"My apologies. I was engrossed in setting up my new laptop."

"The pizza guy came. Seamus called them."

"I forgot all about dinner. Thanks. I'll get some money."

"The boss has it covered."

He pointed to the table. "Do you mind if I bring it

in?"

"No. Please do." She stood and stretched. "I'm starved."

"Well, enjoy it."

"Aren't you going to stay and eat?"

"We have another two pizzas next door."

"We?"

There are three of us over there.

"Oh. I thought it was only you."

"We'll be right through that door if you need anything, ma'am."

"I need you to stop calling me ma'am. I'm not that old yet."

"No disrespect intended." The young man's face turned red. "I didn't think you were old."

"Has anyone ever told you that you look like a young Brad Pitt?"

"My wife has mentioned it a time or twenty."

She chuckled. "You look too young to be married."

"I'm older than Seamus."

Amy felt her ears getting warm. "Really?"

"Yep."

"You have a young face."

"Thank you." He grinned. "I think."

She watched him make his way back to the door. When he reached it, he hesitated with his hand on the doorknob.

"Is there something else?"

He cleared his throat. "It's none of my business, but your wedding came out of nowhere, and Seamus hasn't confided in me as to why, but I know we're here to protect you, so there must be a good reason for it. My guess is the whole marriage thing is part of that, but I don't want to know.

"What I wanted to say is that if you don't love Seamus, you should let him go now. None of us want to see him go through another heartbreak. When he finally got past what Jessica and his brother did to him, he spent the next six months pining over you. If you don't plan to stick around make it clear from the beginning, so he doesn't go through that kind of emotional turmoil again." Trent left and closed the door behind him.

Amy stared at the closed door for a long time before collapsing into a chair at the small table. She'd been determined to dismiss Seamus' claims, but if what the bodyguard said was true, she wasn't being fair. Did she dare hope that he felt that deeply for her?

She opened the box of pizza he'd ordered from her favorite place and smiled when she saw the pineapple and ham. Seamus remembered.

The meeting went longer than Seamus had expected, so by the time he carefully opened the door to the hotel suite, it was quarter past three in the morning. He moved silently so as not to disturb Amy. He needn't have bothered as she sat up in bed wi' her laptop on; her eyes briefly met his before she turned back to what she'd been doing.

He went into the bathroom to get ready for bed, and when he emerged, she hadn't stopped working. "I thought when I left ye behind it would keep ye from spending the night working."

"There is so much to catch up on after our trip. I can't afford to take another break."

"We were only gone for a couple of days."

"Work piles up fast."

"What are ye going to do when we're in Scotland? Do ye plan to spend the entire time glued to yer laptop?"

"Of course not, but I will have to check in and take care of emergencies."

"That is ridiculous. Fractal has a capable staff who kin handle anything that comes up."

"Are you suggesting that I'm not important?"

"I didnae say that."

"It sounded like it to me." She closed the lid on her laptop and set it on the nightstand.

When she flung her legs over the side of the bed to stand, her nightgown rode up, and he caught a glimpse of her bare thigh. He averted his gaze. "I'm sorry I offended ye, but ye let Zach take advantage of ye."

"How can you say that?" She stood wi' her hands on her hips. "He paid for a wedding in Hawaii to help catch my stalker and you think he takes advantage of me?"

"I think that ye care a great deal more for him than ye do yer own well-being."

"Whatever. You don't know anything about it."

"I'm going to get some sleep. Ye should do the same." He hadn't meant to upset her, but she was sensitive when it came to anything involving the boss. He converted the couch into a bed and switched off the light before climbing under the covers. His bed was surprisingly comfortable for a pull-out and it was long enough that his feet weren't hanging off the edge. He could hear Amy moving around in the king-sized bed. If everything went as planned, they could go back to her place tomorrow. The police had determined the blood wisnae human, so there would be no further need to keep the crime-scene intact.

Chapter 7

Seamus' hands tightened on the steering wheel as he listened to Amy's to-do list for the day. "Do ye think ye kin add some time on yer list to go over possible suspects?"

"I thought we did that in Hawaii?"

"We must've missed someone. I need ye to give me an hour, so we kin go through yer old schedules and see who else micht fit the profile."

"Can we do it now? I have an hour before my first meeting."

"Fine. Are ye able to open yer schedule to the beginning of the month?"

"Sure." After two minutes she turned back toward him. "My schedule is open on my screen."

"Read me yer calendar items one at a time and we'll discuss them."

"Is this necessary?"

"Aye."

She began listing her calendar items as he drove. When they reached the parking lot, he pulled into his spot and turned to face her. "Read that last one again."

"Order pizza."

"Do ye always order from the same pizza shop?"

"Yes. It's Zach's favorite, and I enjoy it, also."

"The same shop I ordered from last night?"

"Yes."

"Interesting." He pinched the bridge of his nose. "Dinnae order from them again until we resolve this. Find another pizza shop."

"Seriously?" At his look, she relented. "Fine, but I don't think my stalker is the pizza delivery boy."

"Naw. Doesn't seem likely to me either, but let's not ignore any possibility." He reached for his door handle. "Should we finish this in yer office or mine?"

"Yours. If I go into my office, I'll be inundated with work."

He went around and opened the passenger door for her.

Amy read through her calendar one item at a time.

Seamus looked up from his laptop. "Read that one again."

"It's nothing."

"Humor me."

"Carl Simmons. We bought a messaging app from him; I've only met him a time or two in meetings with Zach. I deal with his assistant most of the time."

"I'm adding him to my list. Something is off wi' that guy. He kept Zach in that meeting last night until two in the morning."

"You're wasting time focusing on him. Long meetings don't mean someone is crazy. He doesn't even know I exist. The guy is probably just a workaholic like Zach."

"If you say so." He typed in the name and gestured for her to continue.

A few names later, he said, "That one sounds promising, as well."

"Jeffrey, my computer support guy?"

"He's a distinct possibility. He could track you through your devices."

"I highly doubt that Jeffrey is stalking me."

"I've seen stranger things."

"Like pizza delivery guys flying to Hawaii?"

"Exactly."

She looked up from her iPad. "I need to get going."

"We're almost done."

"I really have to go."

"I'll walk ye to the conference room."

"I'm capable of getting myself to the meeting."

"Tis my job to keep ye and Zachary safe. Have ye forgotten?" He crossed his arms over his chest. "Besides I need to be in the same meeting."

"Why didn't you say that from the start?"

When they got out into the hall, Seamus took her hand in his.

She rolled her eyes. "You're insufferable."

"Our marriage must appear real, lassie."

Giving in, she leaned into him slightly. Judging by the grin on his face, he didn't mind. She knew she couldn't keep her shields up much longer, so it was imperative he find her stalker soon. Yet, she fought him at every turn instead of helping him find the guy, so they could both move on with their lives. As their head of security, he wasn't leaving, but once her stalker was caught, she wouldn't have to spend every second of every day with him at her side. Maybe that was why she was fighting him. She didn't want to lose him again.

Putting aside the thought, she concentrated on the matter at hand. If her stalker was arrested. They didn't have much on him. They'd only get him for breaking and entering and possibly terroristic threats. He'd be out within hours. It wouldn't due to dwell on that. Even if the law couldn't do much, they needed to find out who was harassing her. Then they could at least get a restraining order. They worked so well for other women. Not.

"How many murdered women have restraining orders against the men who kill them?"

"I'm not certain. Why the morbid question? Dinnae be thinking like that. Ye won't need a restraining order. We'll figure out who's been harassing ye, and we'll put an end to it."

"You honestly think it'll be that easy?"

"Aye. Ye gave me a couple of good leads. I'll look into them."

Seamus opened the conference room door, and

Amy entered wi' a wide grin on her face that he knew wisnae genuine.

Zach stood when they entered the room. "You two are late."

"Apologies, boss."

"Have a seat. We'll recap what we've discussed so far."

After forty-five minutes in the insufferable meeting, Seamus walked Amy to her office and then hurried back to his own. He only had ten minutes before he needed to attend another meeting wi' Zach, and he had some leads from Amy's calendar he wanted to explore. Getting on the phone wi' the company she ordered the company's computer equipment from soon led him to a regular contact that Amy spoke with at least once a month. The man would nae be as wealthy as they'd profiled her stalker to be, but he coudnae ignore the lead. He sent the man's information off to one of his men and asked for a rush background check before he shuffled off to his next meeting.

There were still a few more items on Amy's calendar they hadn't reviewed. Leaving things undone left him feeling unsettled, but in this job he would nae have the freedom he'd had at Garrison Securities. It would take some getting used to, or he'd have to convince his boss that micromanaging didnae work when it came to security. It would be best if he could assign someone else to shadow Zach while he coordinated everything else, but it micht take some finagling for Zach to see that.

He appeared in Amy's office doorway at six-thirty in the evening. "Are ye ready to go home?"

Wi'oot looking up from her computer, she answered, "I have a few more things to wrap up."

"Kin they wait until tomorrow?"

Her hand stilled on her keyboard, and she turned her attention to him. "I'd rather they didn't, but I suppose they'll keep."

"We've been 'ere for twelve hours. I think ye've earned some time away from the screen."

"You're right." She smiled. "Let me save this, and we can go."

"A' richt, lassie."

She took a moment to finish typing something and then closed that program. He watched as her screen switched to email. Her hand stilled, and her face paled. "There's another message from him."

"Let me see." He stood over her shoulder and read the same ominous words he'd read in Hawaii. This time the black roses were a mere gif, but the message was clear. Her stalker didnae want Seamus in her life and was willing to do whatever it took to make certain he didnae have to share Amy wi' him.

What the other man didnae know was that Seamus would nae hesitate to kill to protect the woman he loved. Did he love her? Could it merely be lust or affection? No. He was certain only love would have drug him back to California as much as he disliked the state. Aye. He loved the lass, and he needed to figure out what to do about it.

Amy's lip curled as she sat on the edge of her couch now scrubbed clean of the blood that had drenched it two days earlier. They'd done a thorough job cleaning it.

"We kin get ye a new sofa if ye like?"

She crinkled up her nose. "Yeah. I think a new couch is in order. Possibly paint and a new carpet, too." She stood and turned slowly in a circle. "I think I'll rearrange the furniture. Hopefully, it will keep me from seeing the room the way it was when we got back from Hawaii."

"I—"

"Don't say 'I told you so.'"

"I wisnae planning to."

"Then don't say 'Ah told ye so, lassie.'"

Seamus chuckled. "I would nae do that." He put his hands on her shoulders. "I was going to say, I will be happy to help ye renovate the room."

"Really?" She leaned back slightly and met his gaze. "I could hire contractors and an interior designer."

"It will suit ye better if we do it ourselves."

"I'd like that."

The week flew by as he helped her renovate her living room. Most nights after work, they made trips to stores to choose paint swatches, carpet, and furniture. She wasn't as absorbed in her work at Fractal and found herself watching the clock as quitting time neared. There was something comforting about working side by side with Seamus as they painted her living room, but as the days flew by, he grew distant. Her guess was that their inability to identify her stalker was aggravating him. The trip to Scotland drew near, and, as far as she could tell, they weren't any closer to finding out who was harassing her. The messages had only come by phone and email since they'd returned to her home, and she suspected the tighter security was responsible for the change.

Amy reclined in her seat. They took a commercial flight, but they had seats in first-class. The flight seemed endless. She'd flown around the world with Zach, but on his private jet there was space to roam and escape the other passengers. She'd become overprivileged since she started working for Fractal. An ounce of humility wouldn't hurt her.

Seamus leaned toward her and raised an eyebrow. "You a' richt?"

"I'm feeling guilty for not fully appreciating first-class seats."

His eyes crinkled at the corners. "It is a step down from private flights."

"Are you sure you want to continue this marriage charade when we get to Scotland?" She turned to look out the window before facing him again. "I don't see the point in lying to your family."

"My family is large. Someone will tell someone who will tell someone else. Tis better if we dinnae let them in on the whole story. They'll understand the secrecy when they learn 'twas to protect ye from harm."

She gnawed on her bottom lip. "I hope you're right."

"I am." He grinned. "Dinnae fash yersel'."

They'd been flying for almost fourteen hours with only a brief layover at London's Heathrow Airport when they were asked to put their tray tables up and secure their safety belts for landing. Amy glanced out the window as they approached the runway at Inverness, but even though it was two in the afternoon, the mist was so thick it felt like evening making it difficult to see much. A slightly bumpy landing had her reaching for Seamus' arm. Once they were safely on the ground, she pulled her hand back and stuffed it in her pocket. "Now what?"

"Angus should be here to pick us up. We have a long drive ahead of us." He got their carry-on bags and waited for her to precede him down the aisle.

Amy's hand flew to her chest when the driver brought the car to an abrupt stop on the narrow strip of road. An enormous long-haired beast with enormous horns blocked the path forward. Seamus chuckled.

Her mouth dropped open. "What are you laughing at?"

"Ye are afraid of a cow."

"That thing is not a cow."

"Tis most certainly a cow."

"Those horns aren't normal."

"Certainly, they are." He pointed to a pasture filled with the giant beasts. "Look."

"They don't look like any cows I've ever seen."

"Highland Cattle. They're gentle giants. Ye have nothing to fear from them."

Her eyes widened, and she pushed herself farther back in her seat. "Whatever you say."

"Trust me."

She sighed. "That hasn't worked out well for me thus far."

He clenched his jaw and turned away from her.

Once again, she'd said the wrong thing. "Sorry."

He didn't respond. He just stared out the car's windshield.

The hairy creature sauntered out of the way, and the car lurched forward.

Seamus sucked in a deep breath. "Almost home."

"Home?"

"Aye. Tis home to me."

"I thought you grew up in the states."

"'Twas a mix. I have dual citizenship."

"I didn't know that."

The driver pulled up the long drive, and she stared at the enormous castle towering over them. When the car stopped, the driver opened her door, and she gaped at the stone edifice before her.

"Thanks, Angus. That'll be all." Seamus crossed the distance between them.

"That was weird."

"What?"

"The way you spoke to the driver."

"Was I rude?"

"No. Just authoritative. I felt like we were transported into the 17th century."

"Welcome to Caer Dawien, my home."

"You grew up in this castle?"

"For the most part." He grinned. "We split our time between 'ere and the states, but once Da died we were 'ere most of the time."

Before they reached the door, a man dressed in formal attire took their bags and welcomed them.

"Thank ye, Edmund."

Chapter 8

She couldn't believe they were staying in a real-life castle. The bedroom was large with a white stone fireplace and beautiful tapestries hung on the wall. Staying there was a dream come true. She ran a hand along the stonework on the window and stared out over the courtyard.

The place was amazing, but the sleeping arrangements were far from perfect. They hadn't thought things through. Married people shared a bed. They had no excuse not to be confined in this room together. Her eyes flitted to the bed where Seamus was sprawled out staring at his iPad.

He lifted his eyes from the screen, and she let herself get lost in their depths. His ginger hair curled around the nape of his neck. She shoved her hands in her back pockets to keep herself from touching him.

When she'd learned that he'd brought bagpipes with him. She'd felt like she'd been transported back in time. The man was swoon-worthy even before she'd known he played pipes, but she wasn't sure she'd be able to hold onto her heart seeing him here in his home environment. Who was she kidding?

She'd long ago surrendered her heart to him. She reminded herself he'd left her without so much as a goodbye the last time. That was enough to throw ice water on her fantasies and remind her that he was a man like any other, and that if she let him, he'd crush her heart. Again.

"Would you like first turn in the bathroom?" he asked.

She nodded. "How formal is dinner?"

"Quite."

She went to the closet where she'd hung her outfits and chose her most conservative dress, a fitted black gown. Addison had helped her pick it out for a charity function they'd attended. She hoped it would be appropriate for meeting Seamus' family. Grabbing the rest of her things from the dresser, she hurried into the restroom, and closed the door behind her wishing there was a lock she could turn. A half an hour later, she reentered the bedroom to find him already dressed. Her fantasy was complete. He stood before her dressed in a blue and green tartan kilt. A flush warmed her face. "You're kidding, right?"

"About?"

"You're wearing a kilt? To dinner?"

"We all are."

"All who?"

"The men."

"Oh." She smiled and closed the door behind her. "Do all the men wear their kilts as well as you do?"

He took her left hand in his and held it to his chest. "As long as yer wearing my rings on yer wee finger, I expect to be the only man that captures yer attention."

"Oh my." She leaned into him. "Feeling possessive, are you?"

"Mayhap tis seeing ye in that gown, lassie. I cannae help but want to keep ye to myself."

The thought of spending time alone with Seamus made her giddy but falling for him again would be foolish. He'd likely dump her the minute they caught her stalker. It would do her good to keep some emotional distance.

Seamus' arm slipped around her waist and his hand rested on her hip as he escorted her to the dining room. His touch chased away all thoughts of protecting herself, and she reveled in his closeness, breathing in his masculine scent. In that moment, she'd have given anything to remove the "fake" from in front of "bride." She wanted to belong to the man beside her.

When they arrived in the dining room, the men were all wandering around in kilts just as he'd told her they would be. She'd been to Scottish festivals with her old roommate, so she'd seen men in kilts before, but there was something about being inside a castle in the Scottish Highlands that magnified the effect giving the whole evening a dream-like quality. She smiled at each person as Seamus made the introductions.

A young woman dressed in a flowing green silk gown with hair the same shade of red as Seamus' entered the dining room and made a beeline straight for them. "What's this I hear about ye getting married?" She punched Seamus in the arm and leaned toward Amy for a hug.

Amy returned her hug though she hadn't a clue who the woman was.

"I'm Erica."

The name didn't register, so she awaited further explanation.

"Seamus didnae tell ye who I am?"

She shook her head slightly.

Erica turned to Seamus and pinched him. "How does yer wife not know yer sisters' names? Didnae ye even warn her about us?"

He chuckled. "I didnae want to scare her off."

"If yer sisters kin scare her off than she's not the girl for ye, but I doubt she'll frighten easily." She hollered across the room. "Kay, come meet Seamus' bride."

A dark-haired girl crossed the room and held out her hand. "Tis Kayleigh. Did ye meet the twins yet?" She glanced around. "'Ere they are. Emily and Erin, this is Seamus' bride, Amy." The two enveloped her in a big hug.

She barely had time to catch her breath before a blond girl appeared and hugged her "I'm Heather."

"Another sister?"

"Aye."

"I noticed the other girls have names starting with 'E.' How did you and Kayleigh wind up different?"

"Papa says by the time we came around he got tired of getting the names mixed up and thought it micht help to give us more unique names."

"Did it work?"

"Naw. He calls all of us by the wrong names." She giggled.

Within minutes all six of Seamus' sisters surrounded her, each peeking at her matching wedding and engagement rings.

"Does Seamus have brothers he's hiding from me, as well?"

"He does." A man smacked Seamus on the back. "Afraid I'll steal yer bride, big brother?"

Seamus rolled his eyes. "This 'ere is Alec. He's younger by three minutes. Our other two brothers, Graham and Jamie, are over there with their wives. He lifted his chin toward them."

Seamus had a twin. That seemed like information she should've had before they took this trip. She questioned why he'd neglected to mention it. As an only child, she couldn't begin to fathom what it must've been like to grow up with nine brothers and sisters. She thought back to the many hours they'd spent chatting. He'd said he had a large family with lots of siblings, but he never gave details. She studied his profile as he laughed at something his sister, Ellen, said.

An impeccably dressed woman with pure white hair approached her and folded her into a hug. "Welcome to the family, sweetheart. It's nice to finally meet ye. Seamus has been talking about ye for months. I didnae think we'd ever meet the elusive Amy."

Months. Unlikely.

"Mum, don't smother my wife."

"She's going to have to learn that we are an affectionate family."

"Since when?"

"We've always been affectionate."

"Ye are air-kiss affectionate. Not overwhelm the newcomer friendly. I dinnae know what's gotten into all of ye this evening."

"We're excited that ye finally tied the knot. Though I must say that I'm nae happy I didnae receive an invitation to yer wedding." She studied Amy's figure. "Are ye expecting?"

Amy felt her face heat at the suggestion. "No, Ma'am."

"Then why the hurry?"

"Mum. Please." Seamus' ears turned red and he rubbed the back of his neck.

Mrs. McPherson turned to face Seamus' twin brother. "We need to find a good woman for Alec now, and get him to settle down."

Seamus let out a shaky laugh. "Good luck wi' that."

They sat down at the long table and she forced herself to concentrate on her manners, so she wouldn't use the wrong fork or spill her drink on her groom. She smiled to herself. That might not be the worst thing that could happen.

Amy felt welcomed by everyone. Her stomach roiled. She hated deceiving his kind and loving family. Seamus' reasoning for keeping the truth from his family didn't sit right with her. She wanted to tell them everything.

Seamus walked hand-in-hand wi' Amy up the wide curved staircase leading to his bedroom. When they got up the stairs and out of sight of prying eyes, she pointed a finger in his face. "How did you forget to tell me that you had a twin brother and that you were one of ten siblings?"

"I guess it slipped my mind."

"That's not the kind of thing that slips your mind."

He opened the bedroom door and waited for her to enter before following. "I didnae tell ye because I didnae want ye to panic and refuse to come wi' me."

"I might've."

"I had a feeling ye micht."

She plopped down on the bed and kicked off her shoes. He walked over to the bed and took her hand in his. "I'm sorry."

"No. You're not sorry."

"Och, I'm not. What do ye want me to say, Amy?"

"I don't know." She looked down at the floor.

"Whatever my reasons for not mentioning my siblings, I cannae turn back the clock, so can we move past it?"

She gave a slight nod but didn't look up.

He pulled her to her feet and into a hug.

After a long moment, she pulled away. "We

should discuss sleeping arrangements."

He glanced at the bed. "I guess I'm getting the floor."

"How do we get extra bedding without people getting suspicious?"

"We dinnae get any." He released her hand and plopped down beside her. "I'll make do if ye kin spare one wee blanket and a pillow."

"The castle is drafty, are you sure?"

He leaned over her. "Are ye certain ye dinnae want a kiss goodnight?"

"Positive." Her tongue darted out and moistened her lips, belying her words, but he would respect what she said and try to keep from reading too much into the invitation her body language broadcasted.

He opened his nightstand and grabbed his Bible and set it down on the trunk at the foot of the bed. She tossed him a pillow and blanket, and he made up a spot on the floor to sleep.

"I feel bad about relegating you to the floor in your own bedroom."

"Tis my fault we're in this mess," he said.

"True. You could've told your family you're only protecting a client. They needn't believe the fake marriage lie. I don't know why you brought them into this mess."

"Tis best if nobody knows the truth, but us. My family isnae known for their secret keeping abilities." He stood and moved closer to her. His thumb caressed her neck. "Sometimes, I wish this marriage was real, lass."

"Let's not forget it isn't." She pulled out of his arms, wended her way around the bed, climbed on top of it and scooted her way to the top.

He set up his bedding on the floor and settled down to read his Bible. When he glanced up at the bed ten minutes later, he saw that she read hers, as well. She'd brought a Bible. His heart soared at the thought, but then came back to earth when he considered her icy demeanor toward him. Somehow, he would need to melt her heart before her stalker was caught. She didnae trust him, so he'd have to prove to her that he meant to stick around. How would he prove his trustworthiness while they were living a lie? The mess he'd gotten them into coudnae be easily undone. He stared at the words before him and recognized his own sinfulness. He'd messed everything up. He didnae know a way to fix their relationship, but he would pray about it, and hope that God would make a way despite his failings. He didnae deserve mercy, but God was gracious and micht help him despite his poor choices where Amy was concerned. He needed to make things right wi' her and his family.

Amy adored the sound of bagpipes, but when "Scotland the Brave" awakened her at five o'clock in the morning, she pulled the pillow over her head and screamed into it. Slowly, she moved the pillow aside and sat up. When she put her feet on the floor, she yelped. Standing on the frigid floor felt like standing in the middle of an ice-rink barefoot. Stumbling over Seamus' empty make-shift bed, she made her way to the bathroom to prepare for the upcoming day.

Twenty minutes later, dressed in the coziest outfit she'd brought, she headed downstairs to find Seamus. She found him in the mist-shrouded courtyard with a number of other men. She was pretty sure three of them were Seamus' brothers. Five of the men played bagpipes and two banged on drums. Now fully awake, she sat down on a stone bench to enjoy their music.

A little after six o'clock, she glanced down at her smart watch. Her stomach grumbled and she shivered as the cool mist seeped into her bones. She'd hoped Seamus would have time to give her a tour of the castle and grounds. She closed her eyes and listened to the music. The night before, she'd expected him to kiss her, but he'd respected her boundaries. Her head told her things were better that way, but her heart ached to be closer to him.

Someone tapped her shoulder and she jumped. Erica and Ellen were standing behind the bench. "You scared me," she raised her voice to be heard over the pipes.

"Sorry. We wondered if ye'd like to join us."

She got to her feet. "Sure. What are we doing?"

"Making haggis."

When she scrunched up her face, Erica laughed. "I'm kidding. We're doing some party planning. The laird plans to make a huge announcement on Friday, and he wants to have a grand ball for the occasion."

Ellen smiled. "He's a bit over the top, but in a fun way."

"Did I meet him at dinner?"

"Ye did. Seamus may have introduced him as Uncle Alec."

"Is that who Seamus' twin is named after?"

"Aye." She giggled. "Tis strange since Seamus is the heir."

"Why would Seamus be the heir?"

"My mother is Uncle Alec's only sibling and he had no children, so we're his closest relatives. Seamus is the eldest son, so he's next in line for the inheritance and will be the next Laird Dawien."

She raised an eyebrow. "How does he feel about that?"

"The fact that he hasn't mentioned it to his wife says a great deal about how he feels about it."

Her stomach tightened into knots again. They should tell his family the truth to avoid misunderstandings like this one. "I wouldn't read much into it."

"Tis hard not to." Erica put an arm around her shoulders and steered her to a door she hadn't even seen set into the castle wall. The door took them into a tunnel of sorts which led to a narrow stone staircase. "These are the servant stairs."

"Wow." She ran a hand along the rough stone as they entered the stairwell.

"Uncle Alec's staff dinnae use them, but the castle was built wi' servants' quarters and passageways.

Now tis a fun way to sneak around."

Amy surmised they must've only hired skinny servants. It was a tight fit for her, and she wore a size three.

Chapter 9

Two hours later, Amy saw Seamus at breakfast. She piled her plate with eggs, bacon, and sausage, but skipped the baked beans.

"Hungry?" Seamus chuckled when he glanced at her plate piled with more food than his own.

"You have no idea."

When they finished eating, Seamus pulled her chair out for her, and she stood.

"Would ye like to go for a hike?" He grinned down at her.

"Yes. Please." She took his arm and let him lead her away from the group out of the dining room and into a large kitchen. When they were away from the crowd, he slowed his steps. "I saw ye watching us this morning." He grabbed a backpack from a kitchen stool.

"You sounded lovely."

"We were loud."

"I'll admit, the playing woke me, but I enjoyed the music once I was fully awake."

"I like having ye 'ere wi' me."

"I'm enjoying my time here."

He started walking again, and she fell in step beside him. He directed her out a kitchen door. "There is a lovely trail that goes through the gardens 'n' up into the hills, I thought we'd take it."

She glanced down at her feet, and decided her slip-on shoes were probably up to the task. "I didn't bring hiking boots, but I should be okay in these."

"Yer making a habit of forgetting boots. Yer certain yer good in those shoes?"

She nodded.

"One of my sisters may wear yer size," he said.

She shook her head. "I don't need to borrow boots. I'll be fine in these."

"Let's go then."

They stopped to admire different plants and flowers in the garden as they strolled through it. The garden ended where the forest began, so she followed closely on Seamus' heels as he hiked up a steep narrow pathway. The longer they hiked, the more her legs cramped up and her steps slowed.

He glanced over his shoulder. "Are ye a' richt?" He stopped at a rocky outcrop and waited for her to join him. "Let's rest a while."

"Sounds good." She collapsed on the ground, kicked off her shoes, and massaged her aching feet. When she glanced out over the water a minute later, she noticed the reflection of Caer Dawien in the water's smooth surface. "It's peaceful here."

"Aye. We have a bonnie view of Loch Dawien, lassie. Tis even better from the castle tower. I kin show ye later if ye lik'."

"I'd like that." She closed her eyes a moment before refocusing on him. "Your brogue seems thicker here. It's not the gentle burr I'm used to hearing from you back home. Why don't you talk the same way in the states?"

"My brogue thickens when I'm trying to woo ye, lass, but it's as natural as breathing. Tis harder to speak wi'oot it. Most people in the states wouldn't understand me if I didnae tone it down."

"I didnae ken that." She giggled and lowered her lashes. "May I ask why ye feel the need to woo yer wife?"

His eyes darkened as his hand went to the back of her head. His thumb made circles near her ear, and butterflies fluttered inside her. She fought her desire to throw caution to the wind and give in to him.

"We need to remember we're not a couple, Seamus."

He sighed and dropped his hand. "My mum wants us to have another ceremony while we're 'ere."

"What do you mean? Why?"

"Since she didnae get to attend our wedding ceremony in Hawaii, she wants us to have a second one."

"We can't do that."

"Why not? Tis only for show."

"I don't know, Seamus. Another fake wedding? Isn't that crazy?"

"Everything we've done to this point is crazy, what's one more thing if it makes my mum happy."

"You've lost it."

"Is that a yes?"

"I guess so." She'd never crawl out of the mess they were making.

"Wonderful. Mum is friends wi' the Sutherlands and arranged for us to have the ceremony at Dunrobin Castle after they close to the public on Saturday night." He winked.

"Three days from now?" She felt her face grow warm.

"If it isnae real, what does it matter?"

"I guess it doesn't." She concentrated on her cuticles. "But why not have it here at Caer Dawien? I love it here. There is no point in having the ceremony somewhere else."

"Ye'll love it there, too. It's quite different." His gaze took on a faraway look as he stared out over the water. "It's a French Chateau style."

"All right." She nudged his shoulder with her own, and he wrapped his arm around her pulling her closer to him. "I guess we'll do it. We can't get into this thing any deeper."

"My sisters tricked ye into telling them what ye liked when ye were planning Friday's ball."

"That explains all the questions." One corner of her mouth lifted in a half-smile.

"If I had a real bride, I'd want her to be as easygoing as ye are." He turned to face her and took her chin in his hand. "Ye are gorgeous, and I've wanted to make ye mine since I set eyes on ye. The more time I've spent wi' ye, the more I realize how much I lik' ye. Yer witty, smart, 'n' sexy all rolled into one."

"Is that so?"

"Tis the truth."

"What took you so long to say it?"

"When we met, I'd recently gotten out of a bad relationship." He growled. "'Twas my own fault. I knew she wisnae a believer, but we tried to make it work. After two years, I came to find she didnae truly love me. She desired another. We were only together because she coveted my inheritance, and that was the one thing he coudnae give her."

"That's awful."

"Tis part of why I agreed so readily to Zach's suggestion of a fake marriage. Thought being in close proximity micht let us see if we were compatible before we took a chance."

"Didn't we get to know each other when you were my bodyguard the last time?"

"Nae. Not well enough. I wisnae certain about yer faith."

"Meaning?"

"I knew ye attended church, but I didnae know if ye believed the Bible was the word of God, and I didnae know if ye'd accepted Jesus as yer savior."

She rose to her feet. "Why didn't you come right out and ask me?"

"I feared yer answer." He stood.

"You should've asked." She kicked at the dirt and looked over her shoulder before facing him again. "When did you know for sure that I believed?"

"Last night when I heard ye talking to Graham's wife about salvation."

"All this time you've been trying to get me to open my heart to you again, and you didn't know if we had the slightest chance of making it as a couple. You would've let me fall for you all over again and then, if I wasn't a believer, you would've ended things with me?"

"Aye. I coudnae take a chance with a non-believer again."

"Don't you see how cruel that is?" She stared out over the loch with her hands balled into fists at her sides.

"I'm sorry." He moved closer to her and tugged on her ponytail. "Will ye forgive me?"

She stiffened her spine and turned away from him.

Seamus knew she expected him to head back in, but he turned back to the trail and started back up the narrow path. Amy looked down the trail toward the castle before following him. Once they were a good distance from the castle he stopped. She slammed into him, and he reached out to steady her. "Off in lala land?"

"I guess."

"Are ye angry wi' me?"

"Yes."

Not knowing what to do to ease the tension, he spread out the blanket he'd brought and started unpacking his backpack.

"You brought lunch?"

"I thought ye micht fancy a picnic."

He could see the emotions flicker across her face. She wanted to stay mad, but if he pressed the issue, he could get her to forgive him.

"Ah dinnae ken why ah wis such a fool tae dae whit ah did."

"If you think that thick Scottish brogue is going to win me over—"

"What?"

"You're probably right."

"Would ye care for some bubbly?"

"You brought champagne?"

"Naw. Tis sparkling apple cider."

"Sounds perfect." He poured them each a plastic cup of sparkling cider and handed her a wrapped sandwich. "I dinnae ken what these are. Mum made them."

"I'm sure they'll be good."

"She's not much of a cook, but she kin make a decent sandwich."

They unwrapped their sandwiches and ate in silence.

When Amy finished eating, she lifted her hand to his cheek and ran her hand along the stubble.

"I should've shaved."

"No. I like it."

"Ye do?"

"It gives you that rugged outdoorsy look."

"If ye want to stick to yer rules, ye should nae flirt wi' me, lassie."

"How did I flirt?"

"Dinnae play dumb. Ye ken what ye do to me when ye look at me wi' yearning and touch me like yer doing now." He brushed a stray hair from her face and caressed her neck and jaw line wi' a feather-light touch. "Ye cannae pretend not to feel the intimacy."

He saw something flicker in her eyes before she turned away and let her hand drop to her side.

Leaning over, he whispered into her ear. "When ye decide ye want a real relationship, say the word. I'm no longer the one running away." He deserved her cold shoulder. When he'd left, he'd caused her pain, but he'd thought leaving would protect them both. If he'd have stayed, he would have hurt her more in the long run. He hadn't been ready to give her his heart. Jessica's betrayal had been fresh. He'd gone back to Virginia after his assignment without saying goodbye to Amy first, and he could see now that his choice had been the wrong one. He coudnae blame her for not trusting him but hoped they could move past his mistake before the end of his family reunion. It would nae be easy being around Amy if she didnae want more than friendship from him. Her earlier comments betrayed her true feelings, but he wondered if she'd ever allow herself to let him in again.

Packing up their picnic lunch didnae take long. He started back down the trail, and this time she stayed close to his side instead of following behind. The narrow path made walking side by side a challenge, and she brushed into him on more than one occasion. Every touch sent jolts of pleasure through him. As they neared the rocky overlook where they'd stopped earlier, her foot caught on a root, and she stumbled forward. He caught her, but almost lost his own balance. In the process she wound up in his arms. He stood there holding her unwilling to end the embrace.

"You can release me now. I'm upright."

"I dinnae ken about that."

"Why don't you know about that?"

"Having ye in my arms feels right. I think I'll keep ye here."

She put her hands on his chest and pushed away.

He let out a ragged breath and released her.

Back in the room, Amy sat on the bed propped against the pillows and waited for Seamus to come out of the bathroom. He'd gone in to shower and get ready for dinner. She massaged her feet. She longed to curl up under the covers and go to sleep, but they had a long night of socializing ahead of them. These nightly dinners were merely a prelude of the extravagance to come at Friday night's ball. The laird invited the entire village of Dawien to it.

She didn't even want to think about their wedding on Saturday night. They'd taken her measurements and were altering a gown for the ceremony. The lacy creation had been worn by Seamus' mother, grand-mother, and several of his sisters. The thought of wearing that gown and going through the motions again when it meant nothing left her cold.

She should try again to convince Seamus to tell his family the truth. How could they go through with a wedding ceremony in front of his entire family if they didn't mean the vows they spoke to each other? Vows they would write themselves at his mother's suggestion.

Her eyes filled with tears, but when he came into the room, she gaped at him.

"Is something wrong, lass?"

"Where is your shirt?"

"I forgot to bring it in wi' me."

"You forgot it on purpose. Admit it?"

"If I'd known how frazzled it would make ye, may-hap it would have been intentional, but naw, 'twas a mere oversight."

She jumped off the bed, grabbed her things, and hurried past him into the bathroom, shutting the door behind her. If she didn't get it together, he'd have no doubt as to the effect he had on her, and that would make her even more vulnerable. It didn't matter how good he looked shirtless in a kilt, she needed to remain in control of her hormones.

It took her longer than strictly necessary to get ready. If she stayed in the same room with Seamus for more than a few minutes, she'd be tempted to disregard her own ground rules. It wouldn't be so easy to avoid him at their wedding ceremony. There would be another kiss. She couldn't prevent that, and even if she could, she wouldn't want to. She longed to feel his lips against hers again, but she was sure he'd keep it chaste and sweet the same as before, and when they returned to the states, the fantasy would end, but she'd have the memory of his kisses to cherish.

A blush colored Amy's cheeks. He found her embarrassment adorable, but before he could pull her into his arms, she brushed past him and hid in the restroom. Sharing a room wi' her was far from easy.

When she emerged, his gaze hungrily took in her curves encased in a burgundy gown. She'd swept up her hair and fastened it wi' a fancy comb thing in the back. It looked good, though he preferred her hair down, so he could touch it. Not that he had any business running his fingers through the long silky strands.

"Earth to Seamus"

"Sorry."

"Where were you?"

"Thinking."

"Are you ready to head down?"

"We're already late, so yeah. Let's head down."

She chewed on her bottom lip. "I didn't mean to make us late."

"Tis okay. We won't be the only ones. My sisters are notoriously late for dinner, especially Heather."

He held out his hand and when she placed hers in it, he laced their fingers together. It felt right. He didnae want the week to end, but it would, and he didnae know if at the end of it, she would choose to have nothing more to do wi' him. If he worked hard at being charming and attentive, she micht reconsider giving him a second chance. Then maybe she'd want to continue seeing him when they arrived back in the states. He despised Southern California, but loved being close to her, so he'd taken a calculated risk by taking the job with Fractal Enterprises. He hoped it would pay off.

As they approached the dining room, he pulled her close to his side and leaned down. "I dinnae think I told ye how lovely ye look tonight."

"You didn't."

"Ye look stunning, lassie."

She grinned up at him. "You don't look too bad yourself, laddie."

"Dinnae call me a lad."

She giggled. "Don't worry. You look more like a handsome rogue than a young lad."

"Good." He chuckled. "Otherwise, I'd have to prove my manhood to ye."

"I wasn't questioning your manhood, darling."

"What's this I hear?" Alec came up behind them. "Your wife questioning your manhood? Ouch."

"She wisnae questioning anything."

Alec hurried past them and turned around. He walked backwards and laughed. "That's not how a'm going to repeat the story."

Chapter 10

Amy climbed the narrow steps ahead of Seamus. "It must've been difficult for them to control prisoners they were bringing up to the tower."

"Aye. I'm sure 'twas."

She slowed her steps and turned to face him placing her hands on his chest. "You see, I have the leverage now. One tiny push and you'd fall down the steps backward."

He grabbed her hands and held them at the wrist. "Aye. I'm certain my ancestors were wise enough to restrain their prisoners. Mayhap, I should learn a lesson from them."

"I'm not a prisoner."

Her pulse quickened under his fingertips. "Sometimes ye act like yer 'ere against yer will."

"I cannot think of a place I'd rather be."

"And the company?"

A laugh came from below them a second before Erin came into view. "We thought we heard ye coming up here and thought we'd join ye."

"We?" Amy squeaked the word out past her dry throat.

"Aye." Erin grinned. "Emily is right behind me."

"They don't go anywhere separately," Seamus said.

"Tis nae true." She grinned. "I know ye cannae get along wi' Alec, but Emily and I like each other fine. Yer just jealous."

"Nae jealous. Confused."

"Are we going to go the rest of the way up, or is there a reason we're stopped on the stairs?" Emily asked as she approached them.

Amy's face colored. Seamus released her wrists, and she turned and climbed up the remaining stairs. He followed close behind. "Ye can see the view of Loch Dawien I told ye about." He steered her toward a tiny window above her eye-level.

"It's a little high to see out of."

Emily grabbed her hand and pulled her over to another window the same height that had a bench beneath it. "This is how us ladies have to get a look." Emily climbed atop the bench, and Amy cautiously did the same.

"The view is magnificent. I'm glad we didn't miss sundown."

"This time of year the days go on forever," Erin said.

"Tis about time for the mist to move in," Seamus said.

They stood there looking out over the lake for a few minutes as the sky lit up in oranges, reds, and yellows.

"If ye'll excuse us, ladies. I think my wife was telling me how tired she was before ye arrived, so we're going to head to bed."

Erin giggled. "Have fun."

Amy blushed again, and he chuckled.

Once safely ensconced in their room, he turned to her. "I've wanted to get ye alone all night."

"We were alone on the stairs to the tower."

"We were interrupted." A slow smile spread across his face. "Ye never answered how ye feel about the company?"

"There's nobody in the world I'd rather be with, Seamus."

"How can ye be certain tis Seamus and nae Alec?" Her breath mingled wi' his own.

Her lips parted slightly. "I'm positive it's you."

"How do ye ken?"

"I'd know you anywhere."

He hoped she was speaking the truth. The last thing he needed was another Jessica incident. Although, that wisnae the misunderstanding she'd made it out to be. He wisnae certain his relationship wi' his brother would survive another such betrayal. Focusing on the bonnie lass standing mere inches from him, he caressed her neck and collarbone wi' a featherlight touch. "Now that we're alone, I'm frightened."

"What are you afraid of?"

"I'm scared of crossing a line we should nae cross."

"We've been sharing the same space for more than a week, what makes tonight different?"

"Tis something about being in my childhood home

and having ye 'ere wi' me."

"Don't worry. I have no intention of crossing any lines with you. Remember my 'no kissing' rule?"

"Ye broke that rule yersel' while 'acting' in Hawaii. All bets are off now."

"Then why haven't you kissed me?" She stepped closer to him so that their bodies were touching.

"Ye ken why." He released her hands and turned his back on her.

"No. I don't know why." She put her hand on his shoulder. "Explain it to me."

He tensed up. "If we start kissing, ye know as well as I do, we'll have trouble stopping there." He turned to face her.

Her gaze drifted to the floor and then back up to meet his. He held his arms open. She stepped into his arms and they held each other for some time. She leaned back and looked up at him. "I want to believe we could stop, but you're probably right."

"'Tis going to be a long week."

Amy strolled around the first floor of the castle, exploring each room as she did. She'd expected Seamus to be back from his trip to town sooner. She'd decided to stay behind while he went with his uncle to visit some of the villagers, but as the day dragged on, she began to regret her decision. She stopped to admire a suit of armor in an enormous room with weapons lining the wall and a large space in the center that she assumed was for fencing practice. Nothing about the sport appealed to her. Sensing a change in the atmosphere, she glanced toward the door and saw Seamus standing there. "Hey. How was your trip to the village?"

"Fine, lassie. Just Fine."

"Do you want to go for a walk by the loch?"

"Aye." He held out his hand to her, and she slipped hers into his.

"You seem tense. Are you sure everything went all right on your trip?"

"Aye. 'Twas good."

Seamus was silent for most of the walk, but on their return walk, as they neared the castle, he stopped.

"Did I do something to upset you?"

"Nae."

Seamus twin brother strolled up, and she stuffed her emotions down. It wouldn't do to fight in front of him.

"What do ye think yer doing?"

She turned to Seamus expecting him to answer, but then Alec grabbed her arm. "I'm talking to ye." The moment he touched her; she realized her mistake. She hadn't been walking with Seamus. It'd been Alec playing a trick on her.

"I thought..."

"I know what you thought." His green eyes seared into hers, and then he turned his vitriol on his brother. "Stay away from my wife."

She put a hand on his bicep. "I'm sure he was

just playing a joke on us."

He shrugged off her hand. "Dinnae be naive, lass."

Placing his hand on the small of her back, he guided her inside. When they reached the quiet of the library, he rounded on her. "Ye cannae tell me apart from my brother? We dinnae use the same speech patterns. Our body language is different. We dinnae even use the same cologne."

She fought the tears that sprang to her eyes. "It isn't my fault Alec tried to trick me. What are you so angry about? All we did was walk by the loch."

"I'll bet."

Unable to keep her tears from falling, she sank down onto the settee, kicked off her shoes, pulled her knees up to her chest, and rested her head on her knees to hide her tears from Seamus. It didn't work.

He sighed and stood behind her. "I'm sorry. It's possible that I overreacted."

She sniffled and turned to face him. "I should've realized it wasn't you when he kept giving me one-word answers."

"Are ye suggesting I talk too much?"

"No, but you do string together more than a word or two."

"Would ye care for tea?"

"Sure."

He picked up a phone. "Edmund, would ye have Helen bring tea into the library." He sighed. "I'll build up the fire, and we can stay here until it's time to prepare for dinner."

"I missed you while you were in the village."

He threw a log on the fire. "It didnae look that way when I arrived home."

"Are we going to argue again?"

"No. I'm sorry. I simply dinnae ken how ye kin mistake him for me. The only thing similar about us is our looks. We're nothing alike, and ye claimed ye'd know me anywhere." He reached for the fireplace poker and disturbed the hot coals.

"I'll know better next time. I'm sorry."

"Did ye kiss him?"

She lowered her legs to the floor. "Do you honestly think I would kiss him when I haven't even kissed you since we've been here?"

"Ye believed he was me."

"I didn't kiss him."

"If he'd tried to kiss ye would ye have let him?"

She wasn't sure. It was entirely possible. She'd been more than willing to kiss Seamus the night before, so she might've allowed it. Would she have realized her mistake the second his lips met hers? She hoped so. "Let's not talk in hypotheticals." She sucked in a sharp breath and faced him. "Tell me about Alec and Jessica."

"Where did ye hear about that?"

"Does it matter?"

"Nae. Not much to tell."

"That's a lie, and you know it."

He stared into the fire and spoke softly. "I was away on business when Alec thought it would be funny to cozy up to Jessica and pretend to be me."

"And?"

"She'd just gotten off the telephone with me. I was in Madrid, so there was no mix-up when she crawled into bed with my twin brother."

"I can't believe Alec would do that."

"Neither could I. It's taken me a long time to forgive him."

"What about her?"

"Her betrayal was easier to accept. We'd been drifting apart over faith and, believe it or not, sex. She wanted to rush our relationship, and I wanted to take things slowly. With Alec she found a willing partner. They stayed together for six months before she got bored again."

"I'd never do what she did."

He sat down beside her and took her hand in his. "I believe ye, but sometimes my fears get in the way of reason."

He put his arm around her and pulled her closer. "Let's enjoy each other's company for the remainder of the day." He placed a kiss on the top of her head. She snuggled up to him and inhaled his clean, spicy scent.

Everyone was already seated when they arrived in the dining room, Seamus pulled her chair out and waited for her to sit, so he could push her chair in. When he sat beside her, she rubbed her arms.

"Seamus, Amy is cold, get her a shawl or a sweater," Mrs. McPherson said.

Seamus stood.

"I'm fine. Really."

"Tis fine. I kin run up to the room and find something for ye."

"I don't think I brought anything appropriate."

Erin jumped to her feet. "I'll git ye one of my shawls. A've the perfect one. Tis the MacEwen tartan, so it'll match Seamus' kilt."

Amy felt her cheeks heat with the unwanted attention. "Thank you."

Seamus sat back down and put a hand on her knee, she glared at him until he grinned and removed his hand.

Seamus' mother kept the attention directed on Amy with her next question. "How did ye meet my son, sweetheart?"

At least she could be honest when she answered. "Seamus was assigned as my bodyguard."

The older woman blinked. "How come ye needed a bodyguard?"

"My boss and his wife were in danger, and they thought I might become a target since I'm close to them both."

"I see." Her brow crinkled. "Was my son in danger?"

"Not for long. They got the case wrapped up quickly. He stayed on long enough to make sure the danger was past."

"He's such a gentleman." Mrs. McPherson smiled. "Is that when ye fell in love wi' him?"

Once again, her cheeks burned, and she wondered if she could crawl under the table. They'd never spoken of love, but if she were honest, she'd developed feelings for him soon after they'd met. Strong feelings. The type of feelings that dug in deep and wouldn't let go. Was it love? Perhaps. She didn't know, or if she did, she wasn't ready to admit it to herself. She nodded, not trusting herself to speak.

Seamus draped his arm over the back of her chair. She leaned into him, glad for his comforting presence.

"Amy stole my heart almost from the moment we met."

The words caught her off guard, and she snuck a glance at his face. He said the words to make the relationship look real, but his offhand comments were slipping past her defenses. If she wasn't careful, he'd leave her an even bigger wreck than he had the last time.

By the time dinner ended, she wanted to crawl under the covers and sleep. She couldn't take any more of the emotional turmoil the night had wrought on her heart.

Seamus closed the bedroom door behind them. "Come 'ere."

She met his gaze and weighed her options. She could say no. That would be the smart thing to do. If she went to him, he would wrap her up in his muscular arms, and she'd never want to end the embrace. She couldn't force herself to do the smart thing. She closed the three steps between them, and he pulled her body against his own. She could hear his heart racing, and longed to get closer to him, to kiss him, and give herself to him.

He lifted her chin, so her eyes met his. "Yer gorgeous, lass."

Lowering her gaze to the floor, she avoided eye contact.

"How come ye wilnae look me in the eye?"

"I don't want to think you're only interested in my looks."

"Is that what ye think?" He growled low in his throat. "Believe me, Amy. There's no shortage of bonnie lassies for me to choose from if all I was looking for was a beautiful woman in my bed. 'Twas more than yer beauty that kept ye on my mind the months we were apart."

He closed the distance between them until his lips were within an inch of her own.

The anticipation of his kiss made her knees weak, and she wound her arms around his neck.

"Unless ye object, I'm going to kiss ye 'n' disregard yer ridiculous rules."

She dropped her arms and took a step back. "Maybe, we're getting carried away."

He strode over to the window and looked out into the blackness. "Sharing a room is hard."

She swallowed, walked up behind him, and wrapped her arms around his waist. "Yes. It is."

"I'm not the only one suffering?"

"No. You're not alone."

"Ye'd best release me, lassie, before I lose my last

shred of self-control."

She took a step back. "I'll go and get ready for bed."

"I'll go downstairs for a spell."

"You don't have to leave."

"It would be best if I did." He grinned. "I'll be back before ye wake in the morn."

Seamus left the bedroom and went down to the library. He picked up a leather-bound book, threw another log on the dwindling fire and settled into a wing chair to read. He couldn't concentrate on the words staring back at him. thoughts of Amy invaded his mind. The scent of her sweet perfume surrounded him.

"Do you mind if I join you?"

"I cannae escape ye, so ye micht as well."

"Did you want to escape me?"

He glanced around the room and sighed. "If I cannae have ye, I dinnae want to be around ye."

"I can go back upstairs." Her eyes shimmered, and he knew he'd hurt her again.

"Stay." He took her hands in his. "Please stay."

They sat together for a long time wi'oot speaking. She knew how he felt, and rejected him, so it didnae matter how much he longed to make her his. He'd missed his opportunity.

When her eyes drifted closed, he knelt in front of her and smoothed his knuckles over her cheekbone.

"Lassie, tis time for ye to go back up to bed." When she didnae answer, he scooped her up in his arms and carried her up the staircase to their room. His heart jumped as she snuggled in close to his neck and whispered words he'd longed to hear. If only she'd say them while awake. He struggled to open the door while balancing her in his arms, and she stirred. Her eyes met his as he lay her on his bed, and her arms draped around his neck. She pulled him closer, and he groaned. It would be wrong to let her kiss him in her sleep addled state. He placed a gentle kiss on her forehead, and quickly backed away from the bed and made a hasty exit from their room.

He hurried downstairs and left the castle through a door that led to the courtyard. The cool night air helped calm his raging hormones and turbulent emotions. He wasn't certain how Amy felt about him, not really. Her whispered words were nothing more than sleep talk. For all he knew they could've been meant for another man. He could tell she wanted him, but hoped her feelings went deeper than mere desire. She'd mentioned the hurt he'd caused her when he'd left California, but could that mean her words of love were real, or did it simply mean that her ego hadn't been able to take his refusal to get involved at the time. Did she care for him? On Saturday night, he'd learn the truth. If she loved him like he loved her, her true feelings would be revealed when she read the vows she'd written. If she loved him, she would nae be able to fake her way through them.

Several hours passed before he returned to the

bedroom and crawled into his makeshift bed.

He woke to the sound of bagpipes. He'd forgotten to set his alarm.

Chapter 11

Amy came out of the bathroom freshly showered and dressed. Her smile broadened when she noticed Seamus standing by the closet. "Good morning."

"Mornin', lass."

"What did you want to do today?"

He sat down on the edge of the bed and leaned forward. "I thought we'd take a ride to Dunrobin Castle. Ye micht enjoy seeing it before the wedding."

"Didn't you say they were open to the public?"

"Aye." He winked. "We'll blend in wi' the tourists: watch the falconry display, tour the gardens, visit the museum, and have afternoon tea in the tearoom."

She nodded and smiled. "That sounds fun." Her stomach fluttered at the idea of having Seamus to herself all day. They'd be surrounded by people, but they wouldn't be vying for his attention.

Two hours later, they strolled hand-in-hand through the gardens at Dunrobin. Her nerve endings tingled, and she gave herself to the moment. If he made another advance, she would give in. It was too late to protect her heart anyway. Her fears were turning her into someone she didn't like and making them both miserable.

The wooden benches filled up shortly before eleven-thirty when the falconry display was set to begin. Seamus sat and pulled her down beside him. She scooted closer to make room for another couple. Her pulse sped up, and she tucked her hand in the crook of his elbow.

After the demonstration, they walked toward the tearoom, but Seamus didn't hold her hand or drape his arm over her shoulders. Maybe her decision to give in to his advances had come too late. He might've changed his mind about getting involved with her.

A man gave a slight bow.

Seamus stiffened his spine.

"I heard ye would be announced as the new Laird Dawien at Friday's ball. I wanted to say how happy we ur that ye'll be back home."

"Thank ye, Finlay." Seamus tilted his head back and looked at the sky. "We must be going. We'll see ye Friday night."

As they put some distance between them and Finlay, she tried to keep pace with Seamus. "What has gotten into you?"

"Nothing."

"Is it true?"

"What?"

"What Finlay said?"

"Aye."

"Yer moving back to Scotland?"

"Aye. I plan to."

"When?"

"When the laird dies."

"Is there a reason Finlay thinks that is happening soon?"

"Aye."

"Your Uncle Alec seems healthy."

"He refused treatment for stage four colon cancer." He stopped walking and turned to face her. "'Tis only a matter of time. Could be days, weeks, or months, but it won't be years unless God heals him miraculously."

She placed her hand on his arm. "I'm sorry, Seamus. I had no idea."

"I saw no reason to upset ye wi' it."

"The fact that you don't plan to stay in California seems like a good reason to tell me. Do you have any idea how close I was to giving us a chance?" She ran her fingertips along his jawline. "But I can't do that if you aren't planning to stay in the states. I told you not to make promises you didn't intend to keep, so why did you tell me you would stay? You had ample time to tell me you were leaving." She turned and walked away stopping at a bench twenty-five feet from where she'd left him. Seamus didn't approach her. Her gaze darted over to him, and a sour feeling filled her stomach. Today was supposed to be joyful. The plan to let go of her fears and enjoy being in love was dashed with a few words.

Her thoughts turned to the laird. Seamus was losing a loved one. His uncle was dying. A tightness built in her chest, and she hurried back to where he stood. "I'm sorry."

"For what?"

"Making the moment all about me. You're hurting, and I should've shown more concern for your loss than my feelings."

"If ye would stop running from me, I micht share more."

"I'm not running now."

"Are ye certain?"

She looked him in the eye and smiled. "I am."

The preparations for the ball were complete and Seamus sat in the library waiting to be called. He would enter the room wi' his bride on his arm. Her first introduction to the formalities of life in Caer Dawien. He wondered how she would take to the villagers. Glancing at his watch, he looked toward the door. He couldn't imagine what was keeping her.

As soon as the thought crossed his mind, she floated into the room. She was a vision in a soft-green gown. The diamond jewels she wore highlighted her perfect ears and graceful neck. His throat went dry. "Ye look amazing."

Her smile was tentative. She closed her eyes and lowered her head. "Thanks."

He closed the distance between them and lifted her chin, so she was looking him in the eyes. "Are ye a' richt?"

"I'm fine." A blush rose to her cheeks.

"Why are ye blushing?"

"I'm not."

He raised an eyebrow.

"Maybe I'm nervous."

"I'll be beside ye the entire night."

"I'm sure the village girls will want to dance with you."

"I'm all yers, lassie."

She walked over to the fire, and he followed. His hands moved to her waist and he placed tiny kisses at the nape of her neck.

"Don't start that now. You'll make me blush again, and I'll be frazzled when we have to walk out there in a moment."

"I'd give up being Laird Dawien for ye."

"I wouldn't want you to. This place means everything to you."

"Nae. Ye mean everything to me."

"If ye gave up your rightful place here, you would grow to resent me. Enough of that talk. Let's enjoy the ball."

He turned her to face him, and his hand moved to the back of her head. Lowering his lips to within inches of hers, he stopped and grinned.

Amy held her breath and leaned closer to Seamus anticipating his kiss, but at the last second, he stopped and smiled.

"I think I'll wait for ye to initiate our next kiss, so I ken be certain tis what ye want." He released her and walked over to the bookcase.

She smoothed the front of her dress with both hands, avoiding eye contact with him. Did she have the courage to initiate a kiss? She should follow him across the room and kiss him right now before her nerves got the better of her. No. She would wait until the moment was right.

Edmund appeared in the doorway and motioned for them to follow him.

They stood by the ballroom entrance as Laird Dawien took the stage. "I've an announcement to make."

The room fell silent.

"Many of ye know my health is failing. As of tonight I'll be turning over Caer Dawien and my responsibilities as Laird Dawien to my nephew, your new laird. Please welcome the new Laird and Lady Dawien."

Seamus took her hand and pulled her along beside him. When they reached his uncle, he gave a slight bow, and she curtsied as her sisters-in-law had showed her was proper. "We thank you for the warm welcome. I'll do my best to be worthy of the title." He looked out over the crowd and smiled before tucking her close to his side and heading out into the sea of people.

She tired of trying to decipher the heavy dialect and let herself daydream instead of listening to Seamus converse with the locals. Seamus squeezed her hand. "I dinnae think ye heard a word I said."

"No. I'm sorry." Her hand made a sweeping gesture. "This is a bit overwhelming."

"I didnae know the laird was planning to do that, ye ken."

"You didn't?"

"Nae. My uncle didnae mention it." He shrugged.

"Your sisters mentioned it days ago."

"And ye didn't think to share that information with me?"

"I thought you knew after we ran into Finlay. You didn't seem surprised by his comments."

"Finlay hits the bottle pretty hard. I dinnae take his words seriously." He took her hand in his. "Let's dance." They moved onto the dance floor for a traditional waltz. He was a skilled dancer, so following him was effortless. By the time he led her to a table, her feet were sore from dancing several in a row.

"I can't believe I got you to myself all that time."

"I told ye earlier, I'm all yers."

"I'm sure your adoring fans wouldn't much appreciate that. Go ahead and mingle. I'll rest my feet awhile and talk to Erin and Emily." She nodded toward the twins who were seated nearby.

"Are ye certain? I'm content to stay by yer side all night."

"Go." She pointed to a group of people who looked like they were waiting to speak to him. A minute later she sat down with the twins and they talked nonstop about the excitement of the announcement and how happy they were to welcome her as Lady Dawien. A queasy feeling in her stomach had her excusing herself to get some fresh air.

Seamus watched as Amy slipped out the door into the gardens. It took him a few minutes to make his way through the crowd, but as soon as he could, he followed. Approaching her from behind, he removed the comb that was holding her hair in place and ran his fingers through the silken strands. She leaned back against him, and his arms slid around her waist. "I want ye to be mine, lassie."

She turned in his arms and raised her chin. "You know I'm yours, Seamus."

"For how long?"

"Until it's time to go home and get back to reality."

"Then what happens?"

"Ye come back here and take over your responsibilities, and I go back to work."

"Why?"

"What do you mean why?" She searched his eyes. "What other choice is there? I have a life in America, and you have a life here."

"Why cannae we have a life together?"

"We weren't meant to be."

He wiped a tear from her cheek wi' his thumb. "Do ye believe that?"

Her chin trembled. "I don't know. I've spent my life hearing the Bible verse '... all things work together for good to them that love God...', but sometimes I can't see the good. Why would God let us have this time together just to rip us apart?"

"He also told us we reap what we sow. And in that case, this all seems fitting. But the God I serve is also gracious, long-suffering, and forgiving."

"We messed things up."

"I told ye I choose ye over Caer Dawien."

"I won't let you."

"What can I do to hold on to ye, lass?"

"It'll be easier for both of us, if we accept that we aren't meant to be." She stood on her tiptoes and kissed him, then turned and went inside.

He'd wanted her kiss, and she'd obliged. But the goodbye in her kiss had been unmistakable. His love wasn't enough to hold her, and she'd rejected the idea of him returning to the states wi' her. There was nothing left to do, but make the most of their remaining time together, so he could hold onto the memories. He went back inside and sought her out. He found her giggling wi' his sister, Ellen. He took her by the hand and led her back out onto the dance floor. If she was going to leave, he would make certain she would struggle to forget him.

Amy tried to catch her breath as Seamus spun her around the dance floor. The change in him made her heart ache. An hour ago his eyes held laughter and maybe even love, but now they were cold and hard. Once again, she'd hurt him, but she didn't know how to fix it. They weren't compatible. They lived on different continents. There was no way for them to make their relationship work. Long-distance relationships were doomed to fail.

Besides, he hadn't asked her to stay, not that she could. She didn't know if the United Kingdom would welcome her as a resident or not, and even if they did, what would she do in Scotland. Her home was in California. She loved Seamus, but was that love enough to make it worth the change of culture?

It didn't matter. He'd offered to go with her but hadn't requested she stay. Maybe he didn't think she had what it took to withstand the cool damp weather or the responsibilities she'd have as Lady Dawien. It only made sense that he should choose a girl from the village to marry. It was difficult enough for the locals to accept him when he was half Irish. For him to marry an American was inconceivable, but even as the thought flitted through her brain, she looked around at all the smiling faces of the villagers who'd accepted her as one of their own.

Excuses. That's what they were. Reasons she was giving herself not to stay with the man she loved. Not to take a chance that he might break her heart. Instead she'd broken his, and now all she wanted to do was take back her earlier words and tell him she wanted to stay.

Amy stood in front of the full-length mirror admiring the way the bodice of the ancient lace dress fit her. The experience should be a dream come true.

She was in a fairytale castle in Scotland marrying the man she loved. Again. And it was all fake. A huge deception that was growing more out-of-control every day.

What would his family think of her when this was over, and they learned the truth? They could never have a real relationship after this. It couldn't possibly work. Once they found out the truth, they'd hate her for lying to them. Another deep breath calmed her enough that she could appreciate the smiles of the women surrounding her and return their grins with a tremulous smile of her own.

"I don't know what yer nervous about, Ames." Erin raised an eyebrow.

"My boss is the only one who calls me that."

"Do ye mind it?"

"Not at all. I kind of like it."

"Well, Ames, this is for fun. Ye two did the hard part back in the states. Relax and enjoy yer second wedding day."

She let out a shaky laugh. "We weren't surrounded by Seamus' huge family then."

"Dinnae be nervous. Think of it as another opportunity to spend the night dancing wi' my handsome brother."

A real smile graced her lips. That was one thing she could look forward to. She'd danced with Seamus at the ball the night before and looked forward to being in his arms on the dance floor again.

Erica stood at a window that overlooked Dunrobin Castle's fabulous gardens. She turned to face

Amy. "Are ye ready for this?"

"Not at all."

Ellen laughed. "Get a grip. Ye'v done this before."

"Leave her alone. It must be intimidating for an only child to be surrounded by her husband's whole clan." Heather put an arm around Amy's shoulders. "We're friends not adversaries. It'll be fun. Ye'll see."

Twenty minutes later, she stood in a small room off the drawing room which was decorated for the ceremony. She ran through her vows in her head, but had difficulty concentrating. She put her hand over her eye to stop it from twitching, and as she did so she realized her hands shook.

Mrs. McPherson took her hands in her own and smiled. "I couldn't have chosen a better woman for Seamus if I'd picked ye masell, dinnae let our traditions intimidate ye. This ceremony is for the memories, and I think ye'll be glad of it when the years pass and ye realize ye could've missed this."

"I'm sure you're right." What else could she say?

Before she knew it, she was being ushered to the door of the room. The harp played the first honeyed strains of "Marry Me Now" before the piano and bagpipe joined in. Erin nodded letting her know the time had come for her to begin her walk down the aisle. Her stomach clenched and she bit her bottom lip. Taking that first step, she searched the front of the room for Seamus. When she spotted him waiting for her, tears filled her eyes. Blinking them back, she forced a smile.

Her eyes met his and she held her breath. None of

this was real. If she kept reminding herself that their marriage was fake, maybe she could convince her heart to stop racing whenever he glanced her way.

A jolt went through her when Seamus took her hands in his. She could see by his startled reaction that he'd felt it. Seamus spoke his vows and stared into her eyes with such affection that she longed to believe his words. When her turn came, her mind went blank, so she did the only thing she could do. She spoke from her heart. "Seamus, from the moment I saw you I knew I wanted to spend all my time with you, but it wasn't until I got to know you that I knew I would love you for the rest of my days. The time we spent apart was painful, but it showed me how much I need you. My love for you is stronger than ever. I'm yours now and forever: body, soul, and spirit."

Chapter 12

Seamus listened intently to Amy's words of love and believed them to be true. If she was lying, she was an excellent actress and never should've given up acting to work for Zach. He prayed she wasn't merely performing.

The air sizzled when the preacher told him to kiss his bride. He drew her close and searched her eyes before lowering his lips to hers. He would nae let the opportunity pass wi'oot taking full advantage of it. When her lips parted, he claimed her mouth wi' his and crushed her to him, giving her a taste of the passion he'd been holding back. Their kiss ignited something deep inside that couldn't be quenched wi' a mere kiss. He wanted so much more from her. Ending the kiss, he pulled back and stared into her startled eyes. He supposed she'd expected a chaste kiss like he'd given her in Hawaii, but she'd responded to him wi' fervor to match his own.

He slid his arm around her waist and led her back down the aisle through the cheering crowd made up mostly of his family. The guilt would eat at him later, but for now, he would enjoy the evening wi' his bride. He shouldn't have lied to his family, so he had plenty of regrets, but seeing Amy in that wedding dress wisnae one of them. He bent down and whispered to her. "I hope we kin continue our kiss later." He grinned when her cheeks colored at the suggestion.

"I'm not sure how much more of that kind of kissing we should do." She smiled up at him.

He released her and grabbed his heart wi' both hands. "Ye're killing me."

"I didn't say no." She lowered her lashes flirtatiously. "In fact, I'm hoping we can sneak a few more in soon before we head back to Caer Dawien."

"That's the spirit." When they got to the dining room, he pulled out her chair for her. "Eat light, so I kin spin ye around the dance floor."

Her eyes twinkled when she looked at him. "I'd like that."

"Ye'd better." He grinned. "Yer my bride." He said it for the sake of his eavesdropping family, but her love felt real and he wanted to hold onto it for as long as it lasted. He almost believed she was truly his.

As dinner wrapped up, the music started, and he dragged Amy from her chair and out onto the dance floor. "Ye look breathtaking, lass."

She smiled. "I'm wearing a family heirloom. I hope I'm doing it justice."

"I've never seen it on a more lovely bride."

"You're just saying that."

"Naw. Tis true. Yer gorgeous, lassie."

She blushed again. "Thank you."

His lips brushed against her ear. "If this wedding

was real, I'm not certain I'd make it through the reception wi'oot dragging ye back to Caer Dawien and up to our room."

"Then you best remember this is all pretend." She rested her head on his shoulder and wrapped her arms tighter around his middle.

"I dinnae want to." They could go back to California and get married for real. She'd dismissed the possibility of his staying in California. Would she consider staying wi' him? He'd never know if he didnae get up the nerve to propose. For real.

Later that night, Seamus sat in the courtyard again waiting for his bride to fall asleep. It was going to be another long night.

The laird joined him wi' a Bible in hand. "Mind if I join ye?"

"Not at all." He glanced up at his uncle. "What are ye reading?"

"About how the marriage bed is undefiled."

"What's got ye reading that passage?"

"My nephew sitting in the courtyard on his wedding night."

"Ye would nae understand."

"Try me."

"I cannae." He crossed his arms over his chest.

Uncle Alec clapped him on the back. "If this is about the phony marriage thing, don't fret. There was nothing fake about the wedding ye went through in Hawaii."

Seamus jumped to his feet and faced his uncle. "What are ye talking about?"

"Yer mum suspected something was off, so I contacted yer friend, Grayson. He confirmed our suspicions that yer wedding was supposed to be a bit o' theater, but he discovered that a flight delay resulted in a local pastor filling in for the man who was supposed to officiate yer wedding."

"What are ye saying?"

"The local pastor filed the proper paperwork tying ye to Amy legally."

Seamus sank onto the concrete bench and put his head in his hands. He willed the ringing in his ears to stop.

His uncle went on. "Ye've been married nearly two weeks now, so ye micht as well go 'n' tell yer wife."

"Why didnae ye ask me instead of calling Grayson?"

"I didnae ask ye because ye may have lied again."

He felt like he'd been gut punched, and he deserved it. "Why didnae Gray tell me about the mix-up wi' the pastor?"

"I cannae answer for Grayson, but he may have been waiting until ye got back to the states, so he could tell ye in person."

"What made ye suspect our marriage wisnae real?"

"Yer guilt showed clear on yer face the moment ye arrived. Yer mum asked me to look into it, and I did."

He raked his fingers through his hair. "Mum's going to kill me."

"Yer mum isnae concerned. She sees the love ye share wi' Amy and is glad of it. I'd worry more about yer wife if I were ye. Tis time for the two of ye to decide if ye want yer marriage to last."

"She likes her life in the city. She would be bored here."

"Have ye discussed it wi' her?"

"I asked her once if she thought she'd ever give up her career for a quieter life, and she said 'twas unlikely."

"Go talk to her."

"Wow. We're actually married?"

"Aye. Ye are." His uncle winked. "Tis obvious ye love the lass, so I'd suggest ye remain that way."

"What if she Does nae want me? What if she isnae interested in sharing a life wi' me 'ere in the Highlands?"

His uncle walked to the door and opened it. "I've seen how she looks at ye when she thinks nobody is watching. I believe yer heart is safe wi' the lassie. Give her the opportunity to decide for herself. Ye'll not regret it."

"What about this place?"

"What about it?"

"If I go back to California wi' Amy indefinitely, what happens when—"

"I die?"

Seamus swallowed and nodded.

"I'm not afraid of dying." He sighed. "Yer mum was persistent in making certain I knew where I'd spend eternity. Knowing where I'm going will make it easier to leave my loved ones when the time comes."

"I'm glad." Seamus held back the tears that stung his eyes.

"The plan wilnae change. Yer laird now. If ye cannae be 'ere, have one of yer brothers take care of yer responsibilities until ye kin come home. Alec would be thrilled to be asked."

"I love Alec, but he drives me mad."

"Aye. That's what brothers do. Ye need to forgive him and move past it."

"I have."

"Have ye?"

"I thought I had but seeing him wi' Amy brought up all the old resentments again."

"The anger 'n' bitterness will eat ye alive if ye dinnae let them go."

He sighed. "I know yer right. If Alec takes over temporarily, what happens if I'm gone decades instead of months?"

"Ye'll work it out." His uncle grinned. "I trust ye to make the best decisions for yer future and for the future of the estate. Now, get inside and talk to yer bride, lad."

Amy went downstairs to find Seamus. She had to know where she stood with him, and his running off every time things got difficult wasn't working for her. Relief flooded her when she found him in his usual spot in the library. She held her wedding gown up, so she could move across the floor with more grace. Stopping in front of him, she smiled. "I didn't know where you'd gotten off to."

"A'm here."

She settled on the settee and motioned for him to come over. He quickly abandoned his seat to join her.

"Ye have to stop running away."

"A'm nae running."

"Good."

He took her chin in his hand and lowered his lips to hers. Alarm bells went off in her head. She pushed hard on his chest and rose to her feet.

"Why didn't you tell me you weren't Seamus?"

"Ye didnae ask. I thought ye knew 'twas I."

"You knew perfectly well that I didn't." She moved to the door of the library. "I don't appreciate your games."

She knew she needed to tell Seamus what transpired, but her stomach soured at the thought of doing so. He would be furious when he found out she'd kissed Alec. It only lasted a fraction of a second, but that wouldn't matter to him. He'd never forgive her the transgression. After what happened the other day, she should've been more alert to his brother's tricks, but she hadn't noticed all the little differences. Alec's hair was a fraction shorter, but how was she supposed to notice that in the emotional state she was in. She'd only noticed that he looked exactly like him and was dressed the way Seamus was when he'd left the bedroom. It was stupid of her. They'd worn matching kilts to the ceremony.

Plopping herself down on her stomach atop the bed, she cried until her tears were spent.

Seamus opened the bedroom door to find Amy still in her wedding dress sprawled across the bed on her stomach.

"Kin we talk a minute?"

"Sure." She sat up. "What's up?"

"I have something to tell ye, and I need ye to remain calm."

She crossed her arms. "What?"

"Dinnae get angry."

She scowled. "What makes you think I'll get angry?"

"Ye look like ye micht spit bullets at me if I take a step closer."

"Then maybe you should keep your distance."

"Will ye hear me out?"

"Why not?" She scooted to the top of the bed, so she could lean against the headboard. "What is it you think I can't remain calm about?"

"We're married."

"Well, duh."

"No. Amy, we're actually married."

"No, we're not. You're daft."

"The pastor in Hawaii wisnae the minister Zach hired. He missed his flight, so another pastor filled in, and he wisnae aware of the arrangement. He filed all the appropriate paperwork. Our marriage is official."

"You're serious?" Her face paled.

"Aye." He backed away from her. "I'd hoped ye would nae be terribly upset by the news."

"How did you find out?"

"My Uncle Alec."

"How did he find out? He shouldn't have known our wedding was supposed to be fake."

"Ye are missing the point, lassie. There was nothing fake about our wedding. It was real. We're married. For better or worse."

"For worse than. This is about as bad as it gets."

He opened his mouth to respond, but there was nothing left to say. His lips pinched in a tight line, and he turned to go.

Amy squeezed her eyes shut. She'd said the worst possible thing. Her tongue always got her in trouble, but she'd outdone herself this time. She'd seen the pain in Seamus' eyes before he'd been able to mask it. Now he'd left. Would she be able to find him? He could be anywhere. She ran her hand along the solid carved wood of the bedroom door as tears welled up in her eyes. She pushed the door open, and lifting her gown so she wouldn't trip, she flew down the stairs and into the library, but it was Alec still seated by the fire. She wouldn't make the same mistake again. "Alec, has your brother been in here?"

"Seamus?"

She nodded. What brother did he think she'd be chasing after?

"He came by 'ere. Looked about as wild as a rabid fox. Did ye mention our kiss to him?"

She shook her head.

"The laird led him away before he could break one of his treasures." He glanced around the room at the priceless artifacts.

"Do you know where I can find them?"

"Try the courtyard, but ye micht wish to wait until he calms." Alec frowned. "Seamus has a violent temper."

She'd seen Seamus upset plenty of times before, and he'd never been dangerous. "I need to find him and apologize."

"Good luck."

The words struck her. She didn't need luck. She needed God. A murmured prayer left her lips as she pressed the door to the courtyard open. No Seamus. A shiver skittered up her spine at the eerie feel of the mist shrouding the castle. She trudged back inside and dashed to the kitchen. On her way to the door, she grabbed a shawl from a hook. Cautiously, she followed a path through the gardens to where it split. He could've taken the path they'd hiked together, but she hoped he hadn't attempted it in the dark. For all she knew, he could be somewhere inside, but her heart told her he would've sought fresh air and an escape from the confines of the castle. She took the branch of the trail that led to the loch. Her heels dug into the soft earth, so she kicked them off. They would hinder more than they'd help. The dirt felt cool and damp on her feet. After a short walk she turned a corner and though she couldn't see Loch Dawien through the mist, she knew by the abundance of fog that she'd arrived. She moved toward the solitary shape standing afar off, certain that it was Seamus.

Seamus stood by the edge of the loch, every muscle in his body taut. He caught the scent of Amy's perfume as she approached him silently. He swallowed a dry lump in his throat. He didnae turn to face her. "What are ye daein' out 'ere?"

"I'm sorry."

"Dinnae be sorry. Ye let me ken yer feelings." He sighed. "I'll respect that. We'll get an immediate annulment."

She reached out to him, but he stiffened at her touch and kept his eyes on the mist shrouded loch. His fingernails bit into his fisted palms. He glared over his shoulder, and she dropped her hand. She stood behind him still dressed in her wedding gown.

"I didn't mean what I said." Her voice broke on a sob. "You caught me off-guard. I hadn't expected to find out we were married."

"I saw yer reaction. There is no taking it back, lass. When I learned ye were my wife, I was shocked, but elated. Ye were clearly distraught. I cannae be wi' a woman who doesn't care for me." He turned to face her. "Ye should go to bed and get out of that dress before something happens to it."

"I more than care for you. Seamus, I love you." She dropped down to her knees and sobbed. "Please forgive me and come back inside."

"Get up before you ruin that dress." He didnae wait to see if she obeyed his instructions. If she ruined the gown, so be it. It no longer mattered, he would nae get married again, and he wisnae certain he could let another woman wear it even if he did. He could burn every picture they'd taken at their ceremony, but the image of her in that dress would never be erased from his mind. He turned from her and strode away, determined to put as much physical distance between them as possible.

He kneaded his chest as he walked. Tears burned behind his eyelids, but he would nae let them fall. He refused to give her the satisfaction of destroying him. He never should've agreed to Zach's stupid plan. He'd managed fine alone before, so he would go back to a life wi'oot her and act like nothing had changed. It micht take time, but he'd be a' richt in the end. He walked along the edge of the loch. When he stopped, he could no longer see the outline of Caer Dawien through the mist.

A scream pierced the night.

Chapter 13

A sweaty palm covered her mouth. Her elbow made contact with her assailant's ribs. She screamed again as the man flipped her onto her back. He grunted as he heaved her up onto his shoulder. She clawed at his back, but he didn't react. Branches scratched at her face as he veered off the trail into the woods.

She slammed her fists into his back, but there was no reaction from the brute. Her screams went unanswered, and she prayed that someone knew she was in danger. There was no doubt in her heart that Seamus would do everything in his power to help her if he'd heard her screams.

Stuffing down her rising panic, she prayed. God knew where she was even if nobody else did. If she trusted Him, then she had to know that whatever happened to her, He was in control.

After getting her breathing under control, she forced her body to grow limp hoping her attacker would grow tired from carrying all her weight. It didn't work. He didn't seem to notice a change. After a jarring hike through the woods, he kicked open the door of a one room cabin and tossed her inside. Her face slammed into the hard dirt floor. She sat up and wiped blood from her lip and cheek with the back of her hand. The man gave her a long look before turning away from her and padlocking the door from the inside.

Unsure what the man had in mind, she prayed and poured her heart out to God. The man took a dirty cloth and put it in her mouth, tying it off around her head. Then he took a roll of duct tape and bound her ankles and wrists. He gave her one last look before lying down on a cot in the corner and shutting his eyes. She wondered why he didn't speak. If he was the stalker who'd been harassing her for months, wouldn't he have something to say?

Seamus had gone too far to help Amy. He turned and ran, stumbling on stones and debris along the water's edge. When he reached the place where he'd left her, he found a tartan shawl and a black silk rose. A primal yell tore from his throat.

He hurried inside to seek assistance. He found his brother in the library where he'd left him. "Amy's gone."

"No. She's not. She went looking for you to apologize."

"Her stalker took her. She's gone."

"What are ye talkin' about?"

"I'll explain in the car. We must find her."

"How dae ye ken they drove somewhere?"

"Are ye going to help me or nae?"

"Aye." He stood. "I'll get the keys from Angus."

"I'm going outside to see what I kin find." Inspecting the ground around the circular drive wi' a flashlight, he searched for tire tracks, but didn't find anything that looked fresh. He reckoned there had to be a car involved. The man coudnae made it to Caer Dawien on foot unless he parked nearby and walked the remaining distance. If that were the case, his car may be somewhere on the grounds or nearby. He prayed to God for Amy's safety and promised to release her from her vows if God would keep her alive. He'd walked away when she'd been trying to make amends and had left her alone and vulnerable. He was a lousy bodyguard, but worse yet, he was a rotten Christian. He should've offered her the forgiveness she'd requested instead of being petty about his injured feelings.

Alec honked the horn and Seamus slid into the passenger seat. "Angus is going to wake everybody and organize a search party to check the castle grounds. We'll look elsewhere. Let's go find yer wife," Alec said.

They searched the roadway between Caer Dawien and the village for an abandoned car but found none.

"She's gone, Alec. I lost her."

"Amy's a strong lass, she'll fight back. We'll find her."

He groaned and raked a hand through his hair. "Do ye have any suggestions as to where to look next?"

"Aye." His brother met his gaze. "Let's head back

157

toward home."

"Why? He cannae have gotten to Caer Dawien wi'oot a car."

"I have a thought."

"Are ye goin' to share it?"

"When we were home on summer vacations from boarding school, my girlfriend used to park in a secluded place near the castle, and I'd sneak out at night to meet her."

"Yer point?"

"He micht have parked in the same place. There is a bothy nearby."

"How would he know about that old shelter? I forgot it even existed until ye just mentioned it."

"The location of many of the old bothies is on the internet these days. A simple search would identify the closest ones to Caer Dawien giving yer wife's stalker a perfect hideout right on our castle grounds."

"Let's check it out."

"Before we do, ah need to tell ye something."

"Not now."

"Tis important."

"Nothing is as important as finding Amy."

Alec sighed and turned the key in the ignition. Before long, he pulled his car onto a pull-off that was concealed by the trees. "This is it."

"I dinnae see another car. She's not 'ere."

"There are other places where he micht have parked. We're 'ere, so we micht as well check," Alec said.

Seamus got out of the car and headed toward the bothy.

"I kissed Amy."

Seamus turned to face Alec. "Ye did what?"

"Tonight. It happened fast, I dinnae ken what I was thinking."

"Let's discuss it later."

"She didnae kiss me back."

"Not a surprise if she thought ye were me."

"What do ye mean?"

"When my wife is safe and sound, we can sit down and have a chat, but I cannae have this conversation right now."

Alec started down the path, and Seamus followed. Something hard made contact wi' the back of his head, and he felt himself falling forward. Everything went black.

A noise outside the cabin prompted Amy's assailant to rise to his feet. He gave her a long appraising look. "Where's your rose?"

She didn't know how he expected her to answer with a gag in her mouth.

"I put a rose in your hair before I brought you here." He spit on the ground and then turned to leave. She heard the distinct sound of the padlock this time fastened on the outside. He could leave her here to die. It might be better than the alternatives.

Not ten minutes later, Amy saw a shadow pass by

the window and prayed fervently that if her assailant had returned God would protect her from him. The door jiggled but didn't open. Someone or something slammed into it, but it didn't budge. The man who'd brought her here had the key, so it wasn't him. Dare she hope that it was Seamus?

The shadow returned to the window and she watched as he kicked in the plexiglass and forced his large frame through the small hole. She wanted to shout for joy, but the gag in her mouth prevented her from making any sound. As he approached her, she recognized Alec. He quickly untied her gag and pulled it out of her mouth.

"Are ye a' richt, Amy?"

"Fine. Just get me out of here before he comes back."

"He'll be occupied for a bit."

She tried to search his eyes so like Seamus', but it was too dark to identify much.

"The last I saw him he was dragging Seamus off somewhere."

"You let him take Seamus!" Her voice cracked as she shrieked out the words.

"Calm yersel', lassie. I ken what I'm doing." He scratched the stubble on his chin in a way reminiscent of his brother. It was no wonder she'd mixed them up in the past. "Seamus would want me to get ye to safety before going after him."

"I don't care what he would want." She struggled to get to her feet once the bindings on her legs were cut. "You shouldn't have left him with that monster."

"Dinnae worry about him, I think I know where the man was taking him. Hopefully, we'll get there before he does."

She harrumphed and started to fall, but Alec grabbed her arms and held her up.

"Sorry. The feeling hasn't returned to my legs yet."

"Stomp them. It'll hurt like crazy, but ye'll soon be able to walk."

She did as he suggested while holding onto him to stay upright. He was correct. The feeling came back and pain shot through both legs from her hips to her toes. "Thanks. It worked." She let go of him and moved toward the door.

"We're going to have to leave by the window. Even if we had the key to the padlock it's on the outside of the door."

"If we had a screwdriver, we could take the hinges off the door."

"I don't make a habit of carrying around a screwdriver, do ye?"

"Unfortunately not."

"The window tis then."

He lifted her up and she slid through the narrow space wondering how on earth he'd fit his brawny self through it to get to her. He'd come for her instead of saving Seamus. That had to be a difficult decision. She wasn't sure she could've done the same in his shoes. Leaving his brother must've been scary.

When he got himself through the window, she put her hands on her hips. "Where's Seamus?"

"Yer stalker drug him off through the woods in the direction of the village. If I were to guess, I'd say he was taking him to the cemetery."

"You let him take Seamus to a cemetery?"

"I had to make a split second decision, Amy, and I chose to rescue you first knowing that when Seamus comes to, he'll be capable of defending himself, and he'd kill me if I let anything happen to ye."

"Seamus was unconscious?"

"How else do ye think the man could drag him? Seamus certainly would nae cooperate otherwise."

"How do we get there?"

"We'll take the car." They walked the short distance to where Alec had parked the car, and he got in the driver's door leaving her to go around to the passenger side. He quickly turned the car around and headed toward town but pulled off in a wooded area. "'Tis this way." Alec pointed to a stag trail. "There is nowhere else he could've gone between the bothy and the village."

They hiked into the dark woods by the sliver of faded moonlight barely visible through the dense fog. She followed him down an overgrown trail ignoring the cuts and sores on her feet. Getting to Seamus was all that mattered.

When Seamus opened his eyes, he was flat on his back looking up at the tops of the trees. He said a prayer for Amy's safety, and then rolled over and climbed to his knees. Sharp rocks dug into his bare skin, and he wished he'd taken the time to change out of his kilt. He rubbed at a sore spot on the back of his head. He turned his head to look for Alec, but the movement made him nauseous, so he remained still for a moment. When he next turned his head, the pain was incredible, but he looked around anyway ignoring his agony.

Alec was nowhere to be found. His brother wouldn't have knocked him unconscious. No. The thought was ludicrous. They micht not get along, but his twin brother loved him despite their history.

A shape moved in the distance and he realized he wisnae alone. A large man leaned against an old gravestone about forty feet away. The man was carving something. No that wisnae right. He was sharpening a knife. Ach, that coudnae be good.

"You're awake. Good."

Seamus recognized the voice. Carl Simmons. He'd sat in a meeting wi' him and Zach until the wee hours of the morn. Carl was larger than him, but he wisnae in shape. He was certain if he could disarm him, he'd best him in a fight.

"I didn't want to kill a sleeping man. The idea didn't seem sporting."

"I was unconscious not sleeping." He growled out the words. "Where did ye take my wife?"

"You mean your widow?" The man grinned. "She'll be a widow soon enough. Don't worry about Amy, I'll take good care of her after I bury you. Come see." The man pointed. "Your grave is ready. I dug it out while you slept. You'll stay here with your ancestors for eternity."

Seamus scrambled to his feet and analyzed the situation. He leapt toward the man, pulling his arm behind his back and flicking his weapon to the ground. Wi' one strong push the man landed face first in the shallow grave he'd dug. Seamus heard running footsteps and turned to identify the source. The man grabbed his leg and pulled him down on top of him in the hole. He punched the man in the throat to subdue him.

Alec reached out a hand and helped him out of the grave. "Is he dead?"

"I dinnae think so, but I micht have damaged his windpipe. He'll need medical attention." Seamus' gaze searched behind his brother until he saw Amy. "Ye found her."

"Aye. Yer wife is safe."

"Thank ye." Seamus held his arms open, and Amy stepped into them. He kissed the top of her head. "Thank God yer safe. I've been praying non-stop." She cried softly into his shirt but said nothing. He held her tightly to him and sent up a prayer of thanksgiving.

Alec looked down into the hole. "We need to call for help wi' this creep. He's struggling to breathe. If he doesn't get to a hospital he's going to die."

"Perform CPR, Alec. I can't bring myself to save his life."

"Maybe we should put him in the dungeon and let him die there."

"I dinnae think the authorities would agree wi' that plan."

"It would keep him from stalking and kidnapping women."

"Aye. It would, but it's not the proper way to get justice."

Alec scratched his chin. "Go on home and take yer bride wi' ye. The car is by the road, and the keys are in it."

"What will ye do?"

"I'll do CPR and wait wi' this piece of rubbish until the authorities show up. Don't forget to call them when ye return to Caer Dawien. I dinnae have my cell."

"Me neither. I threw it in the loch the third time Amy called."

"Why would ye do that? What were ye two fighting about anyway? Never mind. Tell me later. Go home."

Seamus bent and picked up Carl's knife that he'd knocked from his hand. "Keep this in case ye need it." He handed the knife to his brother and turned back to Amy. Wi' his arm around her shoulders, they walked out to the road.

Back at the house, all the women greeted them as they walked through the front doors. His sisters took turns pulling Amy into bear hugs. "Thank goodness yer safe," Erin said.

"Are ye a' richt?" Emily asked.

Amy returned their smiles wi' a weak one of her own.

His mum brought Amy and him each a glass of water.

Seamus thanked his mother and his sisters and asked them to call the search off and get the men to come back inside.

When he could break away without offending anyone, he went into the library to escape the noise and pulled Amy in wi' him. He made a phone call before turning to face her. "I need to pick up Alec from the cemetery."

"We can go back for him in a few minutes."

"Nae. I'll go. Ye should stay here and get cleaned up." His eyes darkened as he looked her up and down. "Did he?"

"No. He didn't touch me. The worst thing he did was throw me to the ground. I'll be sore tomorrow and might have some bruises on my face from where I hit the dirt, but I'm okay."

"Do ye think ye'll be able to forgive me for walking away from ye tonight?"

"Yes. Seamus, I'm sorry. My reaction earlier—"

"Dinnae worry about it. I should've understood yer feelings instead of letting my emotions get the better of me."

"You were right to be angry. My words were careless."

"Let's agree that we said some things we regret and argue about who was most at fault later. Go and get cleaned up. I'll be home once Alec and I finish talking to the authorities."

"Aren't they going to want to question me, too?"

"Aye. All the more reason for ye to get yer shower and get some rest before they show up asking questions."

He brushed his knuckles across the red mark on her cheek bone. "Yer scratched up. It'll be bruised for certain in the morn. It makes me want to kill that man for daring to lay hands on ye."

"You almost did."

"Aye. Thankfully, my temper didnae win out. I dinnae need his death weighing on my conscience."

"Seamus?" She put a hand on his bicep.

"What?"

"I need to know we're okay?"

"Aye. We're good, lass." His smile didn't reach his eyes. "Now off ye go." He waited for her to leave before heading back out to the cemetery. The sirens screeched out a loud rhythm as he approached. He found Alec sitting in the back of a police car wi' the door open. "Ye being arrested?"

"Nae. Simply resting."

A constable tapped Seamus on the shoulder, and he turned to face him. After more than an hour of questions, they headed back to Caer Dawien. He hated to wake Amy but knew they wouldn't leave until they spoke to her.

Chapter 14

The last time Amy looked at the clock, it was four-thirty in the morning. The next thing she knew she was startled awake by Seamus sitting beside her and placing a hand on her shoulder. "I need ye to awaken, lass. There is an inspector downstairs with two constables. They have some questions for ye."

She gave him a sleepy smile. "I just remembered that we're married."

"Tis a' richt. I'll release ye from yer vows." He frowned. "I'll be downstairs in the library wi' the inspector. Come down when yer ready."

"Seamus?"

"What?"

"About the marriage—"

"Now is nae the time to discuss it." His shoulders stiffened, and he stood. He moved toward the door.

"Okay." She understood then that he hadn't believed her declaration of love. He thought she wanted to be free of him. Tears stung her eyes as he closed the door behind him. Hopefully, when the police left, she'd have the opportunity to straighten out his thinking.

She drug herself down to the library and sat in

the only unoccupied chair in the seating area by the fire. The inspector peppered her with questions. After answering what felt like hundreds of questions, she felt her eyes drooping. She'd had less than two hours sleep and struggled to concentrate on her answers.

After about an hour and a half, Seamus stood. "If that'll be all, Inspector, Lady Dawien needs her rest."

She felt her face warm when he used the title. It didn't fit her at all. She was nothing more than a fraud.

"Of course." The man rose to his feet, and the two constables did likewise.

Seamus picked up the phone on the desk and hit Edmund's extension. He picked up instantly. "Will you show our guests out, please?" He shook the mens' hands as they left.

When the room was empty of all but Seamus, Amy, and Alec, he sat down across from his brother. "Amy, why dinnae ye head back up to our room. I'll be up to check on ye later." She looked at Seamus and Alec in turn, unsure if she should leave them alone, but chose to do as Seamus asked and headed upstairs.

I didnae forget what ye told me earlier."

"I made a mistake, Seamus. I knew better than to test Amy the way I did Jessica."

"It turned into a lot more than a test wi' Jessica."

"Aye. It did. I thought we were in love."

"Ye slept wi' my girlfriend. Ye moved in together."

"Ye ken I regret falling for her."

"I dinnae ken what ye regret. What possessed ye to go near Amy after everything that happened wi' Jessica?"

"Stupidity. Spur of the moment. I wondered if she'd fall for the childish game we played wi' our girl-friends at university."

"We're not kids anymore, Alec." He scrubbed a hand over his face. "It was silly then to pretend to be each other. Now, it's pathetic."

"It'll never happen again."

"It better not." He met his brother's eyes. "I din-nae ken how ye can expect me to trust ye after that stunt."

"I did rescue yer wife for ye."

"Aye. I forgive ye, but I cannae trust ye. Not yet."

"I understand. For what it's worth, I'm sorry." Alec got up and threw another log on the fire. "What were ye two fighting about?"

"The reason we cannae be trusted either."

"And what is that?"

"Amy and I were faking our marriage."

"Ye aren't married?"

"We are married, but we aren't supposed to be. We both thought our marriage was all for show, but it turned out it wisnae fake after all."

"Why would ye think yer marriage was fake?"

"It was supposed to be, but there was a mix-up wi' the preachers and the fake minister Zach hired didnae show, so we ended up wi' a real preacher."

"Why would ye want to fake a marriage?"

"To trick Amy's stalker."

"Och. Ye were trying to lure him out?"

"We'd hoped he'd give up and go away, but if he didnae leave her alone we hoped to catch him in the act."

"Well, ye did that."

"I'm her bodyguard. It was my job to keep her safe, and I failed."

"Yer more than her bodyguard. The lass is in love wi' ye."

"Ye dinnae ken what yer talking about."

"There would be no doubt in yer mind if ye had seen the state she was in earlier when she thought I let something happen to ye." Alec clasped Seamus on the shoulder and made eye contact. "I messed up, but it won't happen again. I dinnae want to let a woman come between us again. Yer my best-friend."

"I'm yer brother."

"Yer both. I cannae imagine going another year wi'oot speaking."

"We won't." Seamus grinned. "Amy is going back to the states, and we'll get an annulment. Will ye stay and help me run this place?"

"Ye want my help?"

"Aye."

"Of course I'll stay." He stared into the fire.

"Good. It's settled." Seamus stood. "Thank ye."

"Seamus?"

"What?"

"I'm glad yer safe. When I left ye in the woods wi'

that psycho, I was afraid it was the wrong choice, and I micht lose ye. I'm not sure I would've survived the loss."

"Dinnae get emotional on me. Ye made the right choice. I'd have wanted ye to get Amy to safety first." Seamus paused in the doorway to wipe away a tear.

Seamus found Amy sitting up in bed wi' her Bible in her lap. He stood a few feet from the foot of the bed. "I booked an earlier flight. I'll be taking ye home tomorrow morn."

"Why?" She set her Bible down and removed her reading glasses.

"I thought ye micht want to get back to Zach."

"What are ye getting at, Seamus?"

"I'm giving ye what ye said ye wanted."

She got to her feet and put her hands on her hips, her eyes flashing. "Ye never listened to what I wanted."

"Then why dinnae ye tell me what it is ye want, lass?"

Her eyes filled wi' tears and she pushed past him and went into the bathroom, closing the door behind her. He stood next to the door. "What do ye want from me, Amy?" He growled out the question. When she refused to answer him, he left the room.

He found his mother in the parlor. "May I speak wi' ye?"

"Of course, dear. Sit down."

He sat on the edge of a fancy chair and faced his mother. She rang her little bell, and asked Helen to bring the tea service. He waited until the older woman brought the tea and cakes. She filled their cups and left them alone.

"What did ye want to discuss, son?"

"I think ye know."

"I believe I do, but why dinnae ye tell me anyway."

"Last night Amy's stalker found her, so we no longer need to fake our marriage."

"From what yer uncle tells me, yer marriage isnae fake."

"Maybe nae, but it was supposed to be."

"Ye could've told us the truth."

"I should've. I'm sorry."

"Why didnae ye?"

"I wisnae sure everyone could keep the truth quiet, and we were trying to catch this guy, and hoped our marriage micht draw him out into the open."

"It worked."

"Aye. A wee bit too well."

"So, now what?"

"I'm going to take Amy back to California tomorrow and give her an annulment."

"Did ye ask her if she wants an annulment?"

"I didnae have to. She made her feelings clear when I told her we were married."

"Och. I'm sorry to hear that. She made a fine daughter while the marriage lasted."

"I'm sorry I lied to ye, Mum."

"I'm glad ye didnae get married wi'oot inviting yer

family, or rather ye did, but nae intentionally."

Amy filled the tub with cold water and tried to get the stains out of the wedding dress. She couldn't stop her tears from falling, as she looked at the lovely dress covered in dirt and smudged with blood. When she'd worn that dress last night and Seamus had held her in his arms, she'd been so full of hope for the future. She'd thought maybe he'd ask her to stay and they might be able to have the kind of love that Zach and Addison shared.

When the water filled with dirt, she emptied the tub and refilled it with clean water. If only it was that easy to clean up her words. She'd never been good at keeping her thoughts to herself, and now her bluntness had cost her everything. While she'd been thinking about the mess she'd made by mistaking Alec for Seamus and how angry he'd be when he found out, he'd come in and told her the marriage was real. Her comment about it being the worst possible thing was meant in terms of her having to tell her husband she'd mistaken his brother for him and let him kiss her, not that she didn't want him or love him.

She prayed that God would help her learn to think before speaking. A knock on the door, got her attention. "Not now, Seamus, I don't want to fight with you."

"Tis Seamus' mother."

"Mrs. McPherson." Amy opened the bathroom door and found her mother-in-law standing there, looking elegant as usual in pearls and a pantsuit.

"Until yer annulment, ye can call me Mum." She gave her a sad smile. "If ye end yer marriage, ye can call me Maggie."

Amy left the bathroom door open and lifted the soiled dress from the water. "Okay, Mum." She sighed. "I tried to get yer wedding dress clean, but it may be hopeless."

"Nonsense. I'll get the staff to take care of it, and it'll be good as new."

"Oh. I didn't think of that." She hung the dress on a hanger and hooked it over the top shower curtain rod. "Seamus told ye about our marriage."

"He didnae have to, his uncle told me, but I was surprised to learn that ye wanted an annulment, watching ye and Seamus together, I believed ye loved my son."

Amy couldn't stop the tears. "I do love him, but he can't forgive me for saying the wrong thing when he told me we were married. He doesn't believe I love him."

"My boy is a fool. When he asks ye to sign the paperwork, keep in mind that ye have the right to refuse."

"Wouldn't that be wrong?"

"No more so than faking a marriage in the first place."

Amy grinned. "Good point."

Seamus didn't come to dinner and didn't sleep in their room. Amy had an ache in chest that wouldn't ease up. She'd packed her bags before she went to bed, but she kept hoping she wouldn't be leaving. At six in the morning, a knock came at the door. She opened it to find Seamus there unshaven in rumpled clothing. "Why are you knocking?"

"May I come in?"

"Of course." She stepped aside for him to enter.

"Angus is going to take ye to the airport. I've de cided not to fly to the states with ye."

"Oh. Okay."

"I'll get the paperwork for the annulment to ye in the next few days."

Her eyes filled with tears, but she fought them back. "I wish you were coming with me."

"Dinnae do that, lass." He sucked in a breath. "I need to give Zach notice, so I'll be in the states soon, but dinnae worry, I won't force ye to work with me. I'll be coming home as soon as Zach and I can find a suitable replacement for my position. Alec will take care of things here in the meantime."

She put a hand over the ache in her chest. "Why?"

"Because somebody has to take care of things here."

"That's not what I was asking."

"I dinnae know why. I only know that I need some space, so I cannae share a flight wi' ye."

"Okay."

The drive to the airport was silent as she was lost in her thoughts, and she had no idea what Angus must think of her. The flight home seemed endless, and though she tried to read on her Kindle and work on her laptop, she couldn't focus on anything. When the plane landed at LAX, she realized she hadn't arranged a ride home, so she called for an Uber, but when she got to baggage claim she found Zach and Addison waiting there.

Addison wrapped her up in a bear hug, and she sobbed into her shoulder. She reached into her pocket for a tissue and wiped her nose. I need to let the Uber know I have a ride."

"Send Zach to take care of it."

She did, and they stood at the carousel and waited for her bags. Her sister-in-law, Kayleigh, had put ribbons with the MacEwen tartan on the handles of her black bags to make them easier to identify. When she saw one of her bags fall off the conveyor, the tears started again.

"I know you're not crying at the sight of your bags."

"I'm going to miss Seamus' family."

"It's not just his family you'll miss."

She shook her head and the tears started again.

"He'll be back for you, Amy. Give him time."

"No. I messed things up. He won't forgive me."

"I don't believe that."

Chapter 15

Seamus arrived in California two days after he sent Amy home. The ride into work took longer than usual, but it wasn't the traffic that made it feel that way. He expected to run into Amy when he arrived at the office, and he dreaded the confrontation. He had the paperwork for the annulment with him. The sooner she signed it, the sooner he could put this chapter of his life behind him and try to forget that he'd ever known Amy Anderson.

He parked his mustang in the garage and made his way to the top floor of the high-rise where his office was. The elevator doors dinged, and he stepped into the familiar hallway.

Marjorie scowled at him. "What's the matter with you?" she asked, her tone was as rough as her voice. "You have some nerve coming back here after you hurt my girl."

"Good morn, Marjorie." He gave her a half-hearted smile. "And where is Miss Anderson?"

"She's home nursing a broken heart. Zachary has you on his schedule, so you'd best get in there, but don't expect him to be any happier with you than I am."

"Have a lovely day." He walked past her and glanced into Amy's office on his way to Zach's office. His door was open, and he waved him in while he finished his phone call.

"How was Scotland?"

"Dinnae ask."

"Yeah. You broke my personal assistant."

"How exactly did I do that?"

"I'm not sure, but nothing is getting done. I have to rely on Marjorie for everything. Usually, I have to kick Amy out of the office, now I can barely get her to stop in and take care of emergencies."

"I'm sorry to hear she's out of sorts."

"What happened between you two?"

"Gray didn't tell you?"

"He told me about the preacher mix-up. Is that what this is about? It's no big deal. All you need to do is get an annulment."

Seamus held up the folder. "I have the paperwork right 'ere."

"Good. Get it to her." Zach grimaced. "Maybe then she'll come back to work with her head on straight."

A knot formed in Seamus' stomach. An annulment wouldn't resolve what was going on in his own head, but maybe it would help Amy move on.

"I'm giving my notice, Zach."

"No. I won't accept it."

"I'll help you replace me, but I cannae stay."

"Is this about Amy?"

"Nae. I must go home. I have some new responsibilities there."

"This week keeps getting worse." He stood and walked to the windows and looked out over the city. "How soon do you have to go?"

"I can stay for a month or two if ye need me."

"Good. Let's get started on the search right away."

"We need to talk first."

"About?"

"Yer management style."

"Oh?"

"It micht work for the technical side of yer business, but if I help you find a replacement to take over ycr sccurity, you're going to have to put yer trust in them completely. Ye cannae look over their shoulder or expect them to personally attend meetings with ye. They need to be assessing risks and overseeing their employees."

"Okay. Hands-off." He leaned back in his chair. "I get it."

"Do ye?"

"Yeah. I didn't give you the freedom to do your job right and you're afraid I'll make the same mistake with your replacement."

"That about sums it up."

"What about Amy?"

"What about her?"

"What did I do wrong there?"

"Nothing. She loved working for you."

"But I overworked her?"

"I think so, but she's happy with her workload."

"So, when you two run off together, and I'm stuck hiring a new personal assistant, do you think I should try the hands-off thing there, too?"

"Amy and I are not running off together. She's staying 'ere and I'm going back to Scotland."

"I'll believe it when I see it." Zach sat back down and steepled his hands together. "Answer the question."

"It wouldn't hurt for ye to be less micromanaging."

"I appreciate your honesty."

"Does that mean you'll take it to heart?"

"I'll take it under advisement."

"That's all I kin ask."

He headed toward the door.

Zach stopped him before he left. "You two will figure it out. Mark my words."

"'Tis too late for that, Zach."

Amy's doorbell rang, and she set down her laptop and trudged across the room to answer it. Addison stood on her front steps. "Addy, what are you doing here?"

"Nice to see you, too." Addison grinned. "May I come in?"

"Sure." She stepped out of the way to let her friend enter. "Well?"

"Seamus is in the office. I came by to warn you." Addison narrowed her eyes. "He left a folder full of legal documents on your desk."

"You could've called to tell me that."

"I wanted to see how you were doing. Besides, there was something else I wanted to tell you."

"What's that?"

Addison placed a hand on her growing abdomen. "Zach and I wanted you to be the first to know."

"You're expecting?"

"I'm four months along. We're having a girl."

"That's wonderful news." Amy's smile was genuine for the first time since she'd left Scotland. "I'm so happy for you two."

Addison stood. "I have to get back to the office, but I wanted to tell you in person."

"I'll come in."

"Don't, Ames. He doesn't look like he's ready to talk." She sighed. "Work from home today for your own sanity. Please."

She'd hoped that when he arrived in the states, he would have a clear head and be willing to listen to her, but that no longer seemed likely. "All right. I will." She waited until Addison drove away and threw herself on her bed and sobbed until her tears were spent.

Seamus grabbed the folder off Amy's desk and stalked out of the office with it. He was certain Amy's refusal to come into work had something to do wi' him. He'd accepted her feelings about their marriage with as much grace as he could muster, so he didnae ken why she was avoiding him, but if she would nae come to him, she left him little choice but to go to her.

He tossed the folder on the passenger seat and started his Mustang. The motor roared to life and he sped out of the parking garage. His stomach clenched at the thought of facing her, but he had to get it over with, so they could both get on with their lives. There would be another girl eventually. His sisters would see to it that he didnae remain alone long, but he coudnae imagine giving any of them his heart. How could he when it belonged to Amy?

He took a deep breath when he pulled into her driveway. After shutting off the engine, he sat there a moment figuring out what to say to her. Being at her place brought back memories of sitting along the wall surrounding her property and looking down over the hills. It was where he'd fallen for her and where he'd first pulled her into his arms and kissed her.

Letting go was painful but necessary. He'd given the matter over to God. He coudnae keep Amy bound in a marriage she didnae want. He sighed, opened his car door, and trudged up her front steps.

Amy's doorbell rang, and she ran a brush through her hair before answering. It would be Addison checking on her again. She opened the door wide prepared to greet Addy, but Seamus filled her doorway. He held a folder in his right hand. Her heartbeat quickened and she struggled to breathe normally.

He looked her up and down, and she felt self-conscious in her faded jeans and old t-shirt. "May I come in?"

She stepped aside to allow him entry. "Hi."

"Ye hivnae been to work since I arrived back in town. Are ye avoiding me?"

"I am."

"Why?"

"Addison said you didn't look like you were in the mood to talk."

"We don't have to talk, Amy, but I need ye to sign this paperwork."

"No."

"What do you mean, no?"

"I won't sign it."

"Why won't you sign it?"

"I don't want an annulment."

"Why not? It's better than a divorce."

"I want to remain married."

"Yer loopy, woman." He tossed the folder onto her coffee table. "Why would ye want to be married to a man ye dinnae love who lives a continent away?"

"I want to stay married to the man I love, and I want him to take me home with him."

"What about yer reaction the night I told ye we were married? It wisnae a happy one, lass."

"I wasn't upset about the marriage. Your brother kissed me moments before you told me."

"He mentioned that."

"I was stressing over how to explain to you what

transpired between Alec and me when you came in and told me we were married."

"And that made you decide being married to me was the worst thing possible?"

"No, but it made kissing Alec seem so much worse. My reaction was dumb, but it wasn't about being married to you. I love you. Were you not listening when I spoke my vows?"

His eyes darkened. "They were nothing more than a prepared speech."

"No. They weren't. I couldn't remember what I'd written, so I spoke from my heart."

"At the ball, ye claimed ye didnae want me to return to the states with ye. What was that about?"

"I was trying to be fair to you. I understood your need to be in the Highlands, and I thought you would be better off finding a Scottish girl who understood your culture and your traditions. Someone who wouldn't struggle to get used to the constant mist and rain."

"And now?" The corner of his mouth turned up in a hint of a smile. "Ye think ye can learn to deal with mist and rain?"

"I could learn to live in Antarctica if you were there."

"Ye better not be changing yer mind."

"My mind was made up before the ceremony. I tried to tell you when I came to find you at the loch, but you wouldn't listen."

"What should we do with these legal papers?"

"Bring them to Caer Dawien and use them for

kindling in our bedroom fireplace."

"That sounds like a plan I can get behind." He grinned. "Do ye want me to propose?"

"That wouldn't make much sense when we're already married."

"You dinnae want another wedding?"

"Two is more than enough." She looped her arms around his neck.

He lowered his lips to hers, and she melted into him.

Lawfully Guarded

A Free Preview – Trent's Story

Chapter 1

When Alexander Whitaker's office door opened, Trenton Prescott turned his back on the spectacular view of the Pacific Ocean to face the woman entering the room. Her thick brown hair spilled down her back in waves, skimming her waistline. The picture he'd been sent of her didn't do her justice.

Interest sparked in her dark eyes as she looked him up and down. The mini dress she wore showed off her shapely legs, and he fought to keep his gaze on her face.

Delaney Whitaker lowered herself into the chair facing her father's mahogany desk. "What was it you wanted, Daddy?"

"I'd like you to meet Trenton Prescott of Garrison Security."

She turned and appraised him once more before offering her hand, which he shook. "Charmed, I'm sure."

Mr. Whitaker scowled at her. "Trent will be your bodyguard until such time when Courtney is safely returned home, and I determine that the danger is past."

The woman sneered. "I will not be followed around like a child with a nanny."

"You will do exactly what you're told if you'd like to stay in my good graces, my dear." He leaned back in his chair, turning his stare from Delaney back to Trent. "Thank you for getting here so quickly. I appreciate everything Garrison Security is doing to help us during this difficult time."

"Glad to be of service, sir." Trent stood. "If we're about done here, I'd like to get going."

"I think we've covered everything," Mr. Whitaker stood and gave Trent a firm handshake.

The young woman rose to her feet, and the older man kissed the top of his daughter's head, saluted Trent, and left him to face his surly client.

"Well, come on then." Delaney held the door open. "I'll get the staff to ready a room for you."

"We're not staying here." He brushed past her, and the sweet smell of jasmine tickled his nose.

"I'm not leaving home."

He turned to face her. "You don't have a say in the matter, princess. Your father and I worked out the details." He grinned. "You're not safe. Not even in your daddy's Bel Air mansion."

"We have excellent security."

"Yes. So excellent someone managed to get around security, turn off all the cameras, and kidnap your sister."

"My sister is a nitwit."

"Even so, you're coming with me."

"Where are we going?"

"We're staying in a safe-house outside of Seattle."

"Oh joy." She frowned. "My sister is in Seattle, so that's something, anyway." He didn't bother to tell her that she wouldn't see much of her sister while she was there.

He followed her through the state-of-the-art home, walking past a home theater, a wellness center, and a wine room. It would be a challenge for this pampered princess to live with him in a safe house, no matter how well-appointed it was. When they finally arrived on the fourth level and traversed their way to Delaney's bedroom, he stood outside her door while she packed some things. She came out laden with enough luggage for a one-month junket to Europe.

She dropped her bags at her feet and turned to a screen built into the wall. She pressed a button. "I'll need someone to bring my bags out, please."

A man's voice came through the speaker. "Right away, Miss Whitaker."

"I can carry your bags." Trent offered.

"How will you protect me with your hands full, Mr. Bodyguard?" Her words were spoken with seductive undertones. He might've been imagining it, but he didn't think so.

As they passed through the house on their way to the motor court, he admired the infinity pool through the glass on the west side of the house. The house felt more like a pricey hotel than a personal home to him.

Trent assisted Delaney out of the Escalade and onto Garrison Security's private jet, following her inside. She immediately went to the back of the plane where there was a small desk with a mirror. It resembled a make-up table although it was designed as a place for the staff to work away from the main area. He stood discreetly by watching as she reapplied her lipstick and brushed her hair.

When she finally rose to her feet and started back toward the seating area, she spotted him and raised an eyebrow. "Where are my things?"

"The staff loaded your luggage while you spent thirty minutes perfecting your lipstick."

"I did no such thing."

"Maybe it was closer to ten minutes, but you were definitely staring into that mirror back there with a lipstick in your hand."

She settled into one of the luxurious white leather seats. "You were spying on me?"

"I'm your bodyguard." He relaxed into the seat facing hers, stretching his long legs out on either side of hers. "I'm paid to watch you."

"So, that means you must observe me at all times? Even when I'm applying my lipstick?"

"It means when I'm on duty, I will not take my eyes off of you, unless you are in the privy."

"I didn't put makeup on to look good for you." She inspected her perfectly manicured nails.

"Of course not." He chuckled. "We're going to be

around many other people on this private jet." He looked around the empty plane pointedly.

"The pilot might be cute."

"I'm sure her husband thinks so."

Her lips formed a pout and he fought the urge to laugh. Delaney Whitaker was going to be a handful.

"When you're not kidnapping billionaires' daughters, what do you do for fun, Mr. Prescott?"

"Call me Trent, but do you think jokes about kidnapping are appropriate considering the circumstances?"

She blushed. "I wasn't thinking."

He nodded, acknowledging her chagrin, but not making a big thing of it. "My job is what I do for fun." He gave her his most charming smile. "What could be more entertaining than watching young women melt down when they realize their freedom is being restricted?"

Ignoring the jab, she tossed her hair over her shoulder. "You must guard men and children, as well."

"Most of the time I guard men, yes. Occasionally I guard children." He stretched. "Unfortunately, I drew the short stick this time."

"You think you're hilarious, don't you?"

"You don't?" He grinned.

"I think you're annoying."

"Would you like a book to read?" He took a copy of Pride and Prejudice out of the cabinet beside him and held it out to her. "You don't have to waste your time conversing with the staff."

She didn't take the book. "Thanks anyway, but I think I'd rather annoy you."

"Lovely." He set down the book and loosened his tie. "I suppose I should get comfortable then."

"Tell me about yourself, Trent."

"There's not much to tell."

"I'm not sure I believe that." She raised an eyebrow. "How did you come to work for Garrison Security?"

It was an innocent enough question, but, if he wasn't careful, the explanation would tell her much more than he wanted to reveal. "Grayson Garrison and I were in the same unit."

"Unit? As in military?"

"Yes."

"Oh." She flipped her hair over her shoulder. "Did you see combat?"

Visions of war flashed before his eyes. "Yes." He felt a muscle jump in his jaw.

"I can see it's a sore subject."

"It is."

"Let's talk about something else. Tell me about your family."

"My family is great." A genuine smile played at the corners of his mouth. "My father is a real estate developer, and my mother works at his company."

"Any siblings?"

"No. I'm an only child."

"I suppose you never had to fight for affection."

"No, but I would've liked to have a sibling to commiserate with."

"It's not all it's cracked up to be."

"Why not?"

"I love my sisters, but we fought constantly growing up."

"I've heard that is usually the case." He stretched. "What about your parents? I met your father, but what happened to your mother."

"She died when I was young."

"I'm sorry."

"I barely remember her but thank you." She smiled. "Daddy tells us wonderful stories."

He frowned. "I can't imagine growing up without a mother."

"My father played both roles to the best of his ability. Enough about me, where did you grow up?"

"Pennsylvania."

"Wow. Living in California must be so different from where you grew up."

"It would be." He leaned forward. "But I don't live in California."

"Where do you live?"

"Maryland."

"Oh. I assumed you were a local."

"I can live anywhere with my work, but I choose to live near Garrison Security's headquarters."

"Would you ever consider relocating?"

"If circumstances dictated it, then yes."

She leaned back in her seat and closed her eyes. It gave him a chance to study her. Her exquisite beauty was unusual, even a bit exotic. It was a shame she was so far out of his league. Not that it mattered, since she didn't appear to share his values. Yet, there was something about Delaney Whitaker that made him hope to get to know her better.

Trent instructed the driver to bring Delaney's luggage in before leading her toward the kitchen entrance. They continued in and through the kitchen into the open living area before he glanced around the safe-house and turned to face her. "Is this suitable to your taste, Ms. Whitaker?"

She surveyed the room, and he watched as her gaze flitted around taking in the high ceilings, the travertine tile in the entryway, and the fine furnishings. "I'm surprised your boss is able to afford this place. It feels like home."

"Grayson Garrison is worth nearly as much as your father, princess."

"Stop calling me that."

"Nah. It suits you."

"How did a bodyguard get that wealthy?"

"Garrison Security is a subsidiary of Garrison Industries, a global investment firm. Besides, security pays well when you're guarding the wealthy and elite."

"I see." She flipped her hair over her shoulder releasing the fragrance of jasmine into the air. "So, you're being paid well to babysit me?"

"Very well. Would you care to see our suite of rooms?" At her nod, he led the way to the third floor where they would both be staying. The space was more modestly decorated than the downstairs, he wondered what she thought of it. "My room is over there." He pointed. "You'll be staying directly across the hall. We'll share the living area."

"Does that mean I get to sleep in private?" She walked to the door of her bedroom and peered inside.

He walked up behind her and tried to see the room through her eyes. It was a lovely room, but the billionaire's daughter likely had a room fit for a queen back in California. He waited until she turned to face him before he answered. "Yes, you may sleep alone, as long as you promise not to sneak off during the night."

"Now why would I want to leave your company, Trenton?"

He noticed that she hadn't agreed not to sneak off, so he figured he ought to be prepared for her to do just that. "Dinner will be served at seven. Why don't you get changed? I'll meet you in the dining room."

"How should I dress for dinner?"

"Casual is fine."

"Where is the dining room?"

"Take the elevator to the first floor, make a right at the first hall and follow it until you reach the room with the long table."

She nodded before entering her room and shutting the door behind her.

He wondered how he would get through the next several days forced to spend quality time with this over-privileged young woman.

Delaney arrived in the dining room a few minutes late. Trent was already seated, but he stood and pulled out a chair for her. She sat down and a servant placed a steaming plate in front of her. "This looks good."

Trent smiled. "It was a special request. I asked your father what foods you liked."

"That was thoughtful." She speared a piece of lobster and rolled the angel hair pasta onto her fork before taking a bite. "This is delicious."

"I'm glad you like it. I'll let Reggie know."

"The cook?"

"The chef. Yes."

"Please do." She looked down at her plate and then lifted her gaze back to his. "I thought you were going to watch me every minute. How is it that you were down here, while I was upstairs?"

"I said while I was on duty I would watch constantly. Erik is currently on duty." He glanced to the doorway where a man stood guard. She wondered how she'd missed him.

"I didn't even notice him."

"He has a talent for blending into the surroundings and being unobtrusive."

"You could never blend into your surroundings, Trent." She admired his handsome features and the way his hair fell over his eye. She bit her lip, wishing that the attractive man beside her would show the slightest interest in her. His lack of response to her flirting made clear his only interest was in protecting her. Maybe he'd come around if she didn't give up.

"I don't know what you mean?"

"Of course you do." She smiled seductively. "A man as attractive as you could never go unnoticed."

"You'd be surprised, princess." He stood.

"Are we allowed to go for a walk?"

"Sure, but we should stay on the grounds." He held out a hand to her and helped her stand.

"Okay."

He walked with her to the front door. "Are you certain you want to go out there? You might get wet."

"I'm positive." He took his suit coat off and placed it around her shoulders. "That should keep you somewhat dry."

"Thank you." She was touched by his thoughtfulness. They walked down a path across from the house. About five minutes into the walk, they approached a lake. A pair of Hooded Mergansers floated gracefully on top of the water. "This is beautiful." She wiped rain drops from her face.

"It is, isn't it?" His eyes bore into hers before his gaze dropped to her lips, and she wondered if she'd misread him. Maybe he was interested after all.

A fish jumped in the water interrupting the moment. She gave into her desire to play with his hair. "You should be a model." He was close enough that she could smell him, his spicy scent was all male, and she had the urge to pull him close and drink in his fragrance.

A low groan came from deep within him. "Woman, you don't know what you're doing to me."

"I know exactly what I'm doing."

"You're my client."

"I didn't hire you."

"That doesn't make it any more ethical." His eyes turned to look at something, and she noticed Erik standing nearby. "Besides, we're not alone."

"If we were alone, would you have kissed me?" Her eyes searched his.

"You know I would've, but it would've been a mistake."

She sighed. Maybe he wasn't interested in her after all. "Let's go back inside." She walked a few steps in front of him. If he was determined to be nothing more than a bodyguard, then she'd help him out and keep her distance. The idea of staying away from him bothered her more than it should.

Delaney turned on the television but paid no attention to it as she scrolled through her social media feeds. First Facebook, then Twitter, and finally, Instagram. There wasn't much that caught her interest, until she found a post portraying Marc Struck dancing in a Seattle nightclub. The area was only vaguely familiar to her, so she'd have to put the address in her phone's GPS.

When she was comfortable that most of the staff

would be asleep, she dressed and slipped out her bedroom door. She exited through the kitchen grabbing a set of keys from the bowl on the counter on her way.

Once outside she clicked the unlock button and listened to see which vehicle's doors unlocked. Slipping inside the gray sedan, she turned the key, thankful for the quiet engine. A few minutes later, she was safely off the property. It wouldn't do for her to be holed up in a safe house while the rest of the world had fun.

She arrived at the nightclub and searched out her prey. If Trent wasn't interested, she'd find someone who was. A mere hour earlier, Marc Struck had been here, so with any luck he'd still be hanging out. If she could find the Hollywood bad boy and capture his attention, she was certain they'd have a blast together. He'd dated Reagan a few times, before she married Brad. As uptight as she was, it was no wonder the two hadn't made a real connection. No, Delaney was more his type. A free spirit.

After downing her first cocktail, she grabbed a random stranger by the tie and pulled him onto the dance floor. Within a minute, Marc was watching her and within two he'd pushed the other guy out of the way. They danced and drank for hours, having a grand time.

"Come on. Let's get out of here." Marc put his arm around her waist and steered her toward the door.

Her eyes widened in shock when she found the door blocked by several large men.

Another man came up behind her, put his hands on her waist, and pulled her close to him. She recognized Trent's spicy scent, and her traitorous heart did a little skip. He'd come for her.

"Sorry, Mr. Struck, you're going to have to find another date. This little lady is with me," Trent said.

She turned and met his inscrutable green eyes. How had he known where to find her? His hand was splayed across her waist searing into her skin through the thin fabric of her dress. It felt like he'd branded her. The sensation disturbed and excited her simultaneously.

The movie star took a step back and surveyed the group of men. "Sorry, sweetheart." He put his hands up in mock surrender. "You're not worth the trouble."

Delaney cringed at the insult. Maybe Reagan had been right about him after all. She pulled away from Trent and slapped Marc hard across the face. Rubbing her stinging hand she pushed past Trent. "Leave me alone."

"I'm afraid that's not how this works, princess." He slid his arm around her waist. "I'm paid to guard your body. It doesn't much matter to me whether you want me to do my job or not. I will keep you safe with or without your permission."

She pulled away from him. The reminder that he was only doing his job hurt. "You ruined a perfectly good date. I don't want you near me."

"That only makes my work more interesting." He put his hand on the small of her back and escorted her to his car.

"What about the car I drove here?"

"You mean the one you stole?" He opened the car door and waited for her to get inside.

"Yeah. Whatever."

"My men will bring it back."

Once safely inside the vehicle, she let her head fall back against the head rest. Her head was pounding. So much for a good time.

"Do you have any idea how much trouble you could've brought on yourself?"

"I'm not going to stay locked up for the rest of my life."

"Nobody's asking you to remain inside forever, but you need a few days out of the public eye, and then we can devise secure ways for you to go out." He scowled at her a moment before turning his gaze back to the road. "Getting drunk and cavorting with strange men isn't the way to stay safe."

Was that a hint of jealousy she heard in his voice? She wanted to believe it was. "It's a good way to have fun."

"It's a stupid way to have a good time."

"Whatever."

"Aren't you too old for this kind of nonsense, Delaney?"

"You think I'm old?"

"No, but until about four hours ago, I thought you were an adult."

His words cut. He was right, of course. She was behaving like a child. Yet, acting her age seemed beyond her. There was a hole inside that she kept trying to fill, but no amount of partying seemed to fill it.

Trent fell silent. She didn't feel up to starting another argument with him, so she did the same, His honesty offended her far more than the careless insult Marc flung her way. Why should she care what her bodyguard thought of her? He was a paid employee, not a potential suitor. He was nobody. If she could convince herself of that, it would make ignoring his insults easier.

Read More
https://www.amazon.com/Lawfully-Guarded-Inspirational-Contemporary-Billionaire-ebook/dp/B07ML4T1V1/

Dear Reader,

I hope you enjoyed reading my novel, *The Bodyguard's Fake Bride.* If you did, check out some of my other titles. For a list of my current books and upcoming releases check out the novel page on my website: https://www.elleekay.com/novels/

I'd love it if you'd sign up for my newsletter at https://www.elleekay.com/newsletter-sign-up/.

If you enjoyed *The Bodyguard's Fake Bride*, the most helpful thing you can do is leave an honest review. So, please consider submitting a review with the retailer where you purchased this book. It doesn't cost anything other than a moment of your time and can be tremendously beneficial to me. Your quick review helps to get my book into the hands of other readers who may enjoy it.

https://readerlinks.com/mybooks/2115/1/3900

Thank you.
Elle E. Kay
https://www.elleekay.com

About Elle E. Kay

Elle E. Kay lives in Central Pennsylvania. She loves life in the country on her hobby farm with her husband, Joe. Elle is a born-again Christian with a deep faith and love for the Lord Jesus Christ. She desires to live for Him and to put Him first in everything she does.

She writes children's books under the pen-name Ellie Mae Kay.

You can connect with Elle on her website and blog at https://www.elleekay.com/ or on social media:
Facebook: https://www.facebook.com/ElleEKay7
Twitter: https://twitter.com/ElleEKay7
Pinterest: https://www.pinterest.com/elleekay7/
Amazon Author Central:
http://www.amazon.com/author/ellekay
Instagram: https://www.instagram.com/elleekay7/
Goodreads:
https://www.goodreads.com/author/show/1501683
3.Elle_E_Kay

I'd love it if you'd sign up for my newsletter at https://www.elleekay.com/newsletter-sign-up/.

Acknowledgements

A special thank you to my brother, Richard, for coming up with the fictional castle and loch names (Caer Dawien and Loch Dawien) and to my cousin-in-law, David, who came up with the name for a social media platform (Fractal) when I was writing the Billionaire's Reluctant Bride. A big thanks also goes out to my husband, Joe, for putting up with the long hours of writing and editing.

This story is a product of my imagination and a work of fiction. Names, characters, businesses, places, events, locales, and incidents are either the products of my imagination or in the case of actual towns, historical persons, and companies mentioned, they have been used in a fictitious manner. Any resemblance to actual persons, living or dead, or actual events is purely coincidental.

Any errors or deficiencies are my own.

Personal Testimony

I first came to know Jesus as a young teen, but before long I strayed from God and allowed my selfish desires to rule me. I sought after acceptance and love from my peers, not knowing that only God could fill my emptiness. My teen years were full of angst and misery, for me and my family. People I loved were hurt by my selfishness. My heartache was at times overwhelming, but I couldn't find the healing I desperately desired. After several runaway attempts my family was left with little choice, and they put me in a group home/residential facility where I would get the constant supervision I needed.

At that home I met a godly man called 'Big John' who tried once again to draw me back to Jesus. He would point out Matthew 11:28-30 and remind me that all I had to do to find peace was give my cares to Christ. I wanted to live a Christian life, but something kept pulling me away. The cycle continued well into adulthood. I would call out to God, but then I would turn away from Him. (If you read the old testament, you'll see that the nation of Israel had a similar pattern, they would call out to God and He would heal them and bring them back into their land. Then they would stray, and He would chastise them. It was a cycle that went on and on).

When I came to realize that God's love was still available to me despite all my failings, I found peace and joy that have remained with me to do this day. It wasn't God who kept walking away. He'd placed his seal on me in childhood and no matter how far I ran from Him, **He remained faithful.** When I finally recognized His unfailing love, I was made free.

2 Timothy 2:13

"If we believe not, yet he abideth faithful: he cannot deny himself."

Ephesians 4:30

"And grieve not the holy Spirit of God, whereby ye are sealed unto the day of redemption."

I let myself be drawn into His loving arms and led by His precious nail-scarred hands. He has kept me securely at His side and taught me important life lessons. Jesus has given me back the freedom I had in Christ on that day when I accepted the precious gift He'd offered. My life in Him is so much fuller than it ever was when I tried to live by the world's standards.

I implore you, if you've known Jesus and strayed, call out to Him.

If you've never known Jesus Christ as your personal Lord and Saviour. Find out what it means to have a relationship with Christ. Not religion, but a personal relationship with a loving God.

God makes it clear in His word that there isn't a person righteous enough to get to heaven on their own.

Romans 3:10

"As it is written, There is none righteous, no, not one:"

We are all sinners.

Romans 3:23

For all have sinned, and come short of the glory of God;

Death is the penalty for sin.

Romans 6:23

"For the wages of sin is death; but the gift of God is eternal life through Jesus Christ our Lord."

Christ died on the cross for our sins.

Romans 5:8

"But God commendeth his love toward us, in that, while we were yet sinners, Christ died for us."

If we confess and believe we will be saved.

Romans 10:9

"That if thou shalt confess with thy mouth the Lord Jesus, and shalt believe in thine heart that God hath raised him from the dead, thou shalt be saved."

Once we believe he sets us free.

Romans 8:1

"There is therefore now no condemnation to them which are in Christ Jesus, who walk not after the flesh, but after the Spirit."

I hope you'll take hold of that freedom and start a personal relationship with Christ Jesus.

Made in the USA
Las Vegas, NV
24 March 2025

20061547R00132